TOP

OF THE

ORDER

To Kat,

TOP
OF THE
ORDER

JOHN COY

FEIWEL AND FRIENDS
NEW YORK

A FEIWEL AND FRIENDS BOOK
An Imprint of Macmillan

Library of Congress Cataloging-in-Publication Data

Coy, John,
Top of the order / John Coy.—1st ed.
p. cm.
Summary: Ten-year-old Jackson lives for baseball, but becomes distracted
by the approach of middle school, his mother's latest boyfriend, and the
presence of a girl—his good friend's sister—on his team.
ISBN-13: 978-0-312-37329-0 / ISBN-10: 0-312-37329-5
[1. Baseball—Fiction.   2. Friendship—Fiction.   3. Schools—Fiction.
4. Sex role—Fiction.   5. Divorce—Fiction.   6. Family life—Fiction.]   I. Title.
PZ7.C839455Top 2009
[Fic]—dc22
2008028551

Designed by Tim Hall

Feiwel and Friends logo designed by Filomena Tuosto

First Edition: March 2009

10 9 8 7 6 5 4 3 2 1

www.feiwelandfriends.com

For John Kulas,
my namesake

CHAPTER 1

Outside my classroom window, green grass glistens on the first day of May. May means baseball season and baseball season means me. I've been waiting months for this. All the cold, the snow, and the freezing temperatures are gone. Spring's here and I should be on the diamond, not slumped at my desk in Room 106—bored out of my skull.

"There are four hundred and thirty-five members of the United States House of Representatives, and the number of each state's representatives is based on that state's population." Mrs. Spanier pats her nose with a Kleenex. She always seems to have a cold. That's why my best friend Gig named her Snuffy at the start of the year.

I look up at the clock and subtract. Thirty-seven minutes until lunch. Then after we eat, I can be outside smashing pitches to all parts of the field. Our fifth-grade team, the

Panthers, can be good this year, but we need to find some more players.

"Every ten years a census, or counting of the population, is conducted, and congressional districts are altered based on changes in population."

I try to catch Gig's eye, but his head is down on his desk. Snuffy's put him to sleep. I wish we had a different teacher. My friend Isaac has Ms. Kolton, who's fun. Other kids have Mr. Fisher, who doesn't give much homework. Snuffy is the worst—boring and tons of work.

"As the populations in the South and West have increased, states there have gained seats in the House of Representatives. The Northeast and Midwest have lost seats."

Four days until the start of baseball practice. We need to find someone to play second base, my old spot. With Sam Sportelli going out for the traveling team, I finally get to play my favorite position: shortstop.

"Jackson Kennedy, did you hear me?"

"What?" I look up at Snuffy, staring me down.

"I asked you a question about congressional representation, and it's clear you don't have a clue. I suggest you start paying attention, young man."

———

At lunch, I sit across the table from Gig and Isaac as we list what we're dreading about middle school.

"Getting beat up by bullies," Gig says.

"Being jammed in a locker." Isaac grimaces.

"Naked showers after swimming." I dip a mini corn dog in barbeque sauce.

"I heard the pool is full of germs." Gig makes a face. *"Bacteria."*

Isaac breaks his roll in half. "Yeah, they dump so much chlorine in, you smell like pool for a week."

"Eighth graders push you in with your clothes on." Gig points to my tray. "You want that butter?"

"Take it." I thought I was ready for middle school, but now I'm not so sure.

"Then you have to stand butt naked and dry your clothes at the blow-dryer while they snap towels at you and make jokes about how tiny you are." He smears the extra butter on his roll.

That sounds like a nightmare. I'm the youngest of my friends, and the last thing I need is older kids staring and making fun of me.

"And some of the teachers are really mean," Isaac says. "They give you tons of homework and yell a lot."

"They give you detention if you're one second late for class," I add, handing my roll to Gig, who's eyeing it. He's a skinny little guy, but he eats like an all-star wrestler.

"The pressure is so intense that one kid burst his brain," he says.

"No way." I shake my head.

"Uh-huh. His brain burst open right on his desk. My uncle said so. The kid had to go to the emergency room to get his head stitched together. I've seen him. He still has a huge scar."

Isaac bursts out laughing and milk sputters out of his nose.

"You're a human geyser." I laugh, too.

"Did you hear that there's a ghost at Longview?" Gig turns serious. "A girl with long blond hair dropped dead at her locker, and now she haunts the halls."

"There are four ghosts at Eagle Bluff." Isaac holds up his fingers. "A whole ghost family. The school's built on the site of an old airport where a plane crashed into the control tower."

"Kids are just messing with you." I shake my head. "There aren't any ghosts."

"Yes, there are." Gig and Isaac nod like bobble heads.

4

"Did you hear that some eighth graders make you drink a Coke so fast, you hurl in the garbage can?" Gig jams a potato triangle into his mouth.

"Yeah, then they hold you upside down and shove you in," Isaac adds.

"They push your face right into the puke." Gig puts two mini corn dogs up his nose. "I'm Snuffy Spanier." He sniffs and blinks his eyes wildly.

We crack up laughing so hard I'm afraid I'll pee my pants.

"Shh. Here comes the Spaniel now," Isaac whispers.

"Dial down the volume, boys." Mrs. Spanier marches over. She's got pointy glasses and hair that looks like it's glued on.

"We're not that loud," Gig protests.

"You're much louder than the other end of the table." She gestures to a bunch of follow-all-rules girls, who are eating their bag lunches quietly. She gives Gig a pinched-lipped glare. "Spencer Milroy, remove that food from your nose immediately."

Gig takes a nugget out of his nose and pops it in his mouth.

"That's disgusting." She stomps off. "Totally inappropriate."

At the next table, Diego Jimenez, the new kid from Texas, who's sitting by himself, grins.

I notice his Houston Astros jersey. "Hey, Diego. Do you play any baseball?"

"Yeah."

"What position?" He's big and strong.

"Pitcher and first base," he says quietly.

"I'm the number-one pitcher." Gig taps his chest.

"We always need more pitching." I take a practice swing. "Do you bat left or right?"

"Both," Diego says, like he's stating a fact, not bragging.

"Cool. We're playing at recess, and we could use a switch-hitter. Let's see what you can do."

"Okay." He smiles slightly.

"This food is nasty." Isaac crushes his milk carton with his fist.

"That's one thing I heard will be better next year." I push my tray away.

"These aren't bad." Gig pulls the other mini corn dog from his nose, dips it in barbeque sauce, and eats it.

CHAPTER 2

"**A**re you really going to Chickadee Bluff next year?" I turn to Isaac as he, Diego, and I walk onto the asphalt playground.

"Yeah." He flips a baseball into the air.

"Why? You live closer to Longview."

"Yeah, but with open enrollment, you get to choose. My parents think Eagle Bluff is a better school."

I reach over to grab the ball, but he pulls it away from me. Isaac's smart and gets good grades, but that doesn't mean he has to go to Chickadee Bluff. "Longview is just as good."

"My dad is friends with a couple of teachers at Eagle Bluff, and both my sisters went there." He throws the ball high and catches it in his bare hand.

Gig runs up and jumps on my back. "Giddyup." He smells

like cigars from his dad's smoking. Gig is walking second-hand smoke.

I buck him off and he lands in the grass. "Where have you been?"

"Snuffy pulled me aside and gave me one of her safety-first talks." He hops up and imitates her high-pitched voice: "Inserting *foodstuffs* into your nasal passages is an extremely dangerous practice." He sniffs loudly. "I told her it's the only thing that makes school food taste good."

"We've got to persuade Isaac to go to Longview instead of Chickadee Bluff next year." I point at him.

"Longview, Longview," Gig says as we run to catch up with Isaac and Diego.

"Where are you going, Diego?" I ask.

"Longview," he says. "My brother goes there."

"Longview, Longview," Gig chants as we walk across the baseball diamond.

"We're all going to Longview." I wrap Isaac in a headlock. "We can't split up. You and Gig and I have been together since kindergarten."

"I can't help it." He breaks free of my grip.

"Longview, Longview, Longview," Gig and I chant together.

At the backstop, I toss my red bat to Diego to see who hits first. He grabs it halfway down and we all put our hands on top of his. My skin looks pale between his and Isaac's. Gig stretches out his hand, which is speckled with freckles.

Diego smothers the knob of the bat. "I'm up first."

I run out to shortstop and smooth the dirt in front of me. "Throw some strikes, Gig."

"Quit complaining. You haven't seen nothin'." Gig whistles a pitch at Diego's head and he ducks.

Diego steps out of the box and stares at Gig.

"He wasn't trying to hit you," I yell. "He's just a wild thing."

"Shut up." Gig kicks at the mound.

The next pitch is outside and Diego lays off it. He takes a smooth practice swing.

Gig throws one down the middle and Diego smashes a shot. Isaac runs and makes a diving catch in left-center field.

"He robbed you, Diego," I holler.

Diego takes another practice swing.

Gig drops down sidearm and the ball curves over the plate. Diego swings hard and hammers a liner over my head that Isaac chases after.

This guy can hit. "Let's see what you can do from the other side," I shout.

Diego moves around to the left-hand side and digs in. Gig whips a fastball and Diego crushes it to deep center. Over Isaac's head by fifty feet for a home run.

Wow. Nobody in our league has power like that from both sides. I look at Gig, who's watching the ball bounce with his mouth open. "We just discovered our secret weapon."

"Totally." He gives me a thumbs-up.

I walk to the plate. "Diego, we all play on the Panthers in the Suburban Athletic League. You should, too."

"When do you play?" He rubs the sweat off his forehead.

"Wednesday and Friday nights at Echo Park."

"Where's that?"

"Over by the high school."

"I don't know." Diego looks at the ground. "I have to ask my parents."

"We need you." I pound my glove. "Last year, we lost to the Jaguars three times and they never let us forget. With you, we can beat them and get some revenge."

———

After school we swarm out of the building like bees leaving a hive. Isaac stands at the curb in his orange crossing-guard vest.

"I forgot my bus number, mister." Gig jumps up and down and cries like a preschooler.

"There, there, little Giggy. Don't worry." I pat his head. "We'll get you home to Mommy." Kindergartners stand around trying to figure out why a fifth grader is bawling.

"Fank you." Gig bounces around.

Up ahead, Diego's walking to his bus and sorting through some papers.

"Diego, remember to ask your parents," I holler.

He nods but looks uncertain.

"What are you doing after school?" Gig falls back into his regular voice.

"Nothing."

"Come over for dinner. We're having homemade lasagna, your favorite."

"Excellent. I'll ask my mom."

"Hi, Jackson." Gig's sister, Sydney, walks up smiling.

"Hi." She's got brown hair, clear skin, and a computer for a brain. She and Gig are complete opposites. If you didn't know they were brother and sister, you wouldn't guess it in ten million years. Even though they're in the same grade, they're not twins. Gig was held back in kindergarten. Who else do you know who flunked kindergarten?

"Hey, Barf Breath." Gig pulls Sydney's ponytail.

"Cut it out!" She pushes him.

"Gig." I step between them. "Remember, four days until our first practice. We need to find a new second baseman."

"Don't worry. Somebody will show up."

"Not just somebody. We need someone good."

I walk him to his bus and look at all the boys in line: tall ones, short ones, skinny ones, fat ones, some who couldn't hit a baseball if you set it on a tee. Who's going to play second base for us this year?

I wait at the car pickup area with my little brother, Quinn. He's carrying a small clay animal.

"What's that?"

"This is Raffle," he says in his squeaky voice.

"Raffle? What kind of name is that?"

"A good one—for a puppy."

Mom pulls up to the curb in the minivan and unlocks the doors.

"Mom, meet Raffle." Quinn acts like he's introducing her to a person. First graders can be so babyish sometimes.

"Pleased to meet you, Raffle," Mom says. "How are you doing, Jackson?" She looks at me and raises her eyebrows.

"Fine." I slide into the front seat. Mom picks us up on Thursdays and we stay with her until Sunday. She and Dad have joint physical custody—half and half. We've been doing this for two years since the divorce.

"Did you learn anything new today?"

"No." I wave to Isaac as we drive past. "Mom, Gig wants me to come over to his house. Can I?"

"Oh, Jackson, I'm sorry," she says. "I need you to watch Quinn tonight. I have a dinner date."

Another one. I pick at the seat. "Why can't he watch himself?"

"Because he's six, Jackson. Be serious."

"Why can't you get a babysitter?"

"I tried, but everybody was busy. You can go over to Gig's tomorrow night." She checks her watch.

"He didn't invite me for Friday. He invited me for tonight."

"I'll order a pizza and when you finish your homework, you can watch a movie. I'll pay you extra, and I'll take you and Quinn out to Corwin's on Saturday."

CHAPTER 3

"**D**iego." I stumble as I rush to his bus Friday morning. "What did they say?"

"Who?" He squints.

"Your parents. About playing on the team." I brush off my jeans.

"Sorry, I can't play on the weekends." He shakes his head. "I have to work for my uncle."

"We don't play on weekends. I told you we only play on Wednesdays and Fridays."

"What about practice?" He unzips his jacket, showing a MEXICO soccer jersey underneath.

"That's during the week, too. Weekends are free. That's one of the rules." We move toward the entrance with the mob of kids.

"I don't know where it is or how I'd get there."

"Where do you live?"

"Over behind Target."

"We can pick you up. G-Man, my grandpa, usually takes me."

"Why do you call him G-Man?" Diego holds open the door for me.

"He wants to be called that. He says he's too young to be called Grandpa." I rub my hands together. "So you can play then?"

"Maybe. I guess so."

"Great. You're a Panther." We pound fists. "What kind of work do you do anyway?"

"Roofing. My uncle has a crew. I scoop up shingles and load them into a dumpster."

Babysitting Quinn and watching a movie sounds way easier than that.

"Good morning, Diego. Good morning, Jackson." Principal Maroney waves. She's tall with short blond hair and round glasses, and even though she's the principal, everybody likes her.

"Good morning," we both reply. When I was little, I thought it was amazing that she knew each kid's name. I still think it's pretty cool.

"Later." Diego and I split up to go to our rooms.

"Isaac!" I run to his locker. "We've got our secret weapon. Diego can be on the team."

"Awesome." He's wearing blue-and-orange Nikes that match his sweatshirt. As usual, he looks sharper than any of the rest of us. He pulls his math book out of his backpack. "We still need a second baseman, though. My dad said to ask some guys. How about Kai?"

"Kai? He doesn't play baseball anymore. Totally into skateboarding."

"But he still knows how to play," Isaac says. "There he is."

We race down the hall together.

"Slow down, boys." Snuffy, who's coming out of the library, catches us.

"Kai." I walk up fast. "We need a second baseman. Will you play?"

"Nah." He takes off his Tony Hawk hat and shakes his curly hair. "I'm not into the whole team-sports thing."

"C'mon," I plead. "We need you."

"I'd rather skate than have some coach yell at me."

"My dad doesn't yell," Isaac says.

"No thanks." He sets his board in his locker. "I've got better things to do."

"Forget it," Isaac says. "There's Rosario. Let's ask him."

Rosario spins a basketball on his finger effortlessly.

"Hey, R," I say. "We need a second baseman. Will you do it?"

"No, I'm concentrating on basketball this year." He's wearing brand-new white Adidas.

"You can still play other sports." I follow the spinning ball like I'm hypnotized.

"Not if I want to make the sixth-grade team at Eagle Bluff." He flicks the ball.

"That's next year," Isaac says.

"I need to focus on hoops. I don't have time for distractions."

"Baseball isn't a distraction." I shake my head. "Forget it." I turn to walk away. "What about Trenton?"

"Trenton?" Isaac frowns. "He's obsessed with comics."

"I know, but he used to play. I can't think of anybody else."

Trenton is sitting on the floor at his locker, paging through a Batman book.

"We need a second baseman and our first game is in a week. We can't find anyone." I sound like I'm begging. "Will you do it?"

"Baseball?" Trenton looks at us like we just asked him to dance naked on a cafeteria table at lunchtime.

"Yeah, baseball," I say.

"Baseball is so dead.

"No, it's fun. Really."

"Right." Trenton goes back to his book.

Isaac rolls his eyes at me. "I told you."

"What's going on?" Gig's sister, Sydney, comes up behind us. She's with her best friend, Kelsey Neeley, who's also smart and popular.

"We need a second baseman for the Panthers," I explain. "Our first practice is Monday. Do you know anyone who can play?"

"Possibly." Sydney nods. She likes being in on everything.

"Who?"

"I'll check it out." She smiles. "I'll let you know."

After school, Gig and I resume our marathon home-run contest at his house.

"Quit throwing junk." Gig swings his gold Wiffle ball bat.

I pitch the plastic ball and he belts a high fly that just clears the wooden fence in the neighbor's yard.

"Ninety-three to eighty-five," Gig calls. "I'm way ahead."

I pick up another ball and put some spin on it. Gig swings and misses. "Strike." I pump my right arm out. "You're out of there."

Gig flips the bat down and I rush in to pick it up.

"You're going down," Gig shouts.

I stand over the Frisbee we use as home plate and take a practice swing.

Gig floats a ball that's way outside.

"Come on. Give me something to hit." I tap the plate.

The next pitch is down and away, but I swing hard and the ball shoots off my bat. It smacks against the bottom of the fence. Not quite high enough.

I look up at the deck where Sydney and Kelsey are watching. They're wearing matching Hollister T-shirts and they've rolled up the sleeves.

"What are you doing?" Sydney says.

"What does it look like?" Gig picks up another ball.

"Can we play?" Sydney brushes her hair back behind her ear.

"No way." Gig twirls the ball in his hand.

"We both play softball," Kelsey says.

"Big deal." Gig spits. "Softball's for girls."

I look back at Sydney and Kelsey, who are leaning over the top rail of the deck. For a moment I think it's too bad he didn't say yes.

"Ninety-three to eighty-five," he calls. "You'll never catch me."

Saturday morning at the park, I move to my left to scoop up a fast grounder, but the ball skips off my glove.

"Stay down on it," G-Man calls. He's Dad's dad and he's serious about baseball.

"Bad hop." I pick up a rock and toss it aside.

"If you stay down, you have a chance to recover, even on a bad hop." He hits another one that skims the surface.

I stay low, dig it up, and fire to the backstop.

"That's the way."

G-Man, who's wearing jeans and a long-sleeved T-shirt, hits me another grounder. I pay attention to the bounce, scoop it up, and throw it in. This is the same way we practiced when I played second, but it feels better at shortstop. The field looks different from this side. Right-handed batters pull the ball more to short. It's my favorite spot on the diamond, and I'm secretly glad Sportelli is gone so I can play it this year. Grounder after grounder—G-Man and I have been practicing this way since I was five.

"Break time." G-Man waves me in. He pulls two bottles of water out of his mini-cooler and hands me one.

"Thanks." I wipe the sweat off my forehead with my shirt and take a big drink. G-Man was a great player when he was younger. So good he played in the minor leagues.

"I can't believe we're the only ones here." He looks around at the four diamonds. "When I was your age, these fields would have been swarming with kids on a Saturday."

I take another long drink.

"Your arm is stronger this year." He hands me a frozen Snickers. "Are you thinking about going out for the traveling team?"

"I'd rather play with my friends from school on the Panthers." I unwrap the candy bar.

"Sportelli's going out. You know him and you'd make other friends."

I take a bite. The cold candy bar tastes good.

"You could handle it." G-Man rubs his short dark hair that's starting to go gray on the sides. "You should think about it."

"Okay." I nod, but I don't want to change my mind.

"Good." He takes a sip of water. "I finally made that trade online this morning for that McGovern-Eagleton button I was telling you about."

"What did you have to give up?" G-Man collects old things, including political buttons. He's got hundreds in display cases in his basement.

"A packet of Jimmy Carter for President peanuts from 1976. Carter was a peanut farmer from Georgia, and in the primaries, he gave out packets of peanuts with his name and picture on them. The peanuts have held up pretty good. I still have a few of them."

"Could you still eat them?"

"Maybe, but they're more valuable if the package isn't opened."

I take the last bite of Snickers and crumple up the paper. "You're the reason my middle name is Carter, right?"

"Yup," he says. "Once your mom and dad decided on Jackson, I lobbied for Carter as a middle name. Jackson Carter Kennedy—three Democratic presidents. It's a great name."

"I like it."

"Good. That's what counts." He reaches into his shirt pocket. "I got the guy to throw this into the deal." He hands me a red, white, and blue Kennedy button. "JFK. From 1960. I thought you should have it."

"Thanks." I turn the old button over in my hands. It's kind of cool to have the same last name as a president.

G-Man grabs the fence and stretches out his bad knee. "We need to get back to work. I'll hit some in the hole. Practice moving to your right and planting your back foot to throw."

I run out to shortstop and lean forward on the balls of my feet as I breathe in the smell of fresh-cut grass. G-Man cracks a grounder and I take two steps, stretch my glove out, and grab it. I set my right foot and launch a rocket that rattles the backstop.

"Strong throw," he says. "You're ready for the traveling team."

Chapter 4

"Ted's considerate and polite. He's a good listener and very successful." Mom passes me her pasta primavera at Corwin's Grill. "Try this."

"No, thanks." I pick up another sweet potato fry. She makes it sound like Dad is none of these.

"Why are your fries orange?" Quinn looks at my plate.

"Because they're from sweet potatoes, not white potatoes."

"Can I try one?" He leans forward in the booth.

"Sure." I slide my plate over.

"They're good. Can I have another one?"

"Give me some of yours and I'll give you some of mine."

"Ted is an actuary, and he's been giving me tips on expanding my interior-decorating business."

"What's an act-cherry?" Quinn asks.

"It's a job that involves numbers. Ted calculates insurance

25

iums. He's very good at it. He also has two

eleven and Haley is six. I think it would be

.. ιo get together. What do you think?" She smiles

at me.

"I've got baseball." I bite into my cheeseburger. We've gotten together before with the kids of guys Mom's dated, and it's always uncomfortable. The adults watch the kids to see if they get along, like it's a sign that everything will work out. If Mom's excited about dating some new guy, that's fine, but she doesn't have to drag us into it right away.

"Okay," says Quinn.

Mom leans over and gives him a hug. "That's my Quinny. We'll pick a time that doesn't interfere with baseball, Jackson. I know how important that is to you."

I push fries around on my plate. Having your mom dating is a huge pain.

"**H**ey." I walk into the living room, where Quinn steers a miniature police car through a tower of blocks.

"You want to play?" He looks up eagerly. "This is the car wash. Police cars need to look clean."

I sit down and push a fire engine around the shiny wood floor. This room is huge with a grand piano in the corner and floor-to-ceiling windows that look out over the lake. But it's not our house. It belongs to Liz and Jeff, friends of Mom's, who are in Italy for a year. We're house-sitting, which is like babysitting, except for a house. Even with some of our stuff here, it doesn't feel like home.

"The fire station is over there." Quinn points to some red blocks. "See the fire dog."

I pull the fire engine next to the Dalmatian.

"I wish we could get a dog," Quinn says.

"You know Mom's allergic to dogs."

"Yeah, but maybe at Dad's." He adds some blocks to the fire station.

He's a strange kid. He'd rather build a huge city with blocks than play baseball or watch TV.

"All the buildings have sprinkler systems so the fire engine doesn't get called out very often," he adds.

He's really smart for a six-year-old, though. He was only four when Mom and Dad got divorced. I'm not sure how much he remembers them being married. He might not remember our old house on Burnside Lane with the huge maple tree in the backyard where we had our tree fort. He might not even remember the morning we all sat in the family room and Mom and Dad calmly announced they were getting a divorce and said it was nobody's fault. I remember trying to listen to what they were saying, but what I really wanted was to run away and get a chocolate-dipped ice cream cone from Dairy Queen. I still think of the divorce and dipped cones together. I never get that kind anymore.

"Quinn, are you really okay with getting together with Mom's new boyfriend and his kids?"

"Sure."

"Do you know his last name is Bear?" I add an orange triangular piece to the fire station.

"Really?"

"Yeah. And his middle initial is E. That stands for Empty."

"That's not his name."

"Yes, it is. Ted E. Bear. Mom said we can call him Teddy." I push the fire engine into the station as Quinn watches me. He always goes along with Mom. I'm not like him. I'm not very good at pretending I'm interested in something when I'm not.

Sunday, when Dad picks us up in the Subaru, G-Man's sitting up front with him.

"I got my new suit this morning and I'm ready for that big slide," he says.

"Really?" Quinn smiles. "Will you go down, too, Dad?"

"If your grandpa does, I will."

Dad's got our bags with our swimming stuff on the backseat. We usually go to the Y after he picks us up at Mom's. It's like he thinks it's too sudden for us to go straight from her house to his.

"How was your weekend?" he asks.

"Good," Quinn says. "Mom's got a new boyfriend."

He might be smart for his age, but there's still lots he doesn't know.

"Well, she needs to make her own mistakes," G-Man says.

Dad stares at him.

"Choices," G-Man says. "She needs to make her own choices."

Dad catches my eye in the rearview mirror. "How are you doing, Jackson?"

"Okay."

"Have you thought more about the traveling team?" G-Man asks.

"Yeah." I take a deep breath. "I want to play with my friends."

"But you'd make new friends on the traveling team. It would be an opportunity to compete against better opponents, to get better coaching, to play against teams from other suburbs."

I can tell by his tone that he's disappointed. "I like being on the Panthers with my friends."

"But how much better will you get playing with them?"

"If Jackson wants to stay on the Panthers," Dad says, "that's his choice."

"I know it is," G-Man says gruffly, "but if he could make the traveling team, he should try out. Sometimes you have to challenge yourself."

"And sometimes you have to do what you want," Dad says.

I stretch the strap on my backpack. Sportelli says lots of guys on the traveling team are hard-core. The coaches are intense and expect you to dedicate your life to baseball. Besides, the traveling team has tryouts. I might not even make it.

Dad brakes at the crosswalk for a woman walking her poodle.

"Oh, cute," Quinn says. "Dad, can we get a dog?"

"A dog is a lot of work, a lot of responsibility," Dad says.

"Jackson and I will do everything. Feed it, walk it, scoop up poop."

"Speak for yourself." I give him a nudge.

"What about when you're at your mom's and I'm at work?" Dad says. "Who would take care of a dog then?"

"I didn't think about that," Quinn says quietly as he stares after the poodle.

"Dad, wait!" I search through my backpack. "I forgot my glove at Mom's."

"Oh, Jackson." He exhales a long breath.

"Sorry."

"We'll turn around and go back," G-Man says. "You can't play without your glove."

I squeeze my hands together. It's hard sometimes keeping track of things in two different houses.

At the Y, G-Man runs with Quinn to the slide. G-Man's wearing long trunks with green and yellow flowers, like he's come from Hawaii. They look ridiculous.

"No running." The lifeguard whistles them down.

Quinn and G-Man scamper up the ladder. Quinn goes first and lies flat on his back as he slides around the curves. He splashes into the water and paddles like an otter to the side. "Your turn, G-Man."

G-Man lies back and dunks into the water with such a

big splash that his swim trunks start to slide off. He grabs them and ties them tightly while the lifeguard shakes her head. "Almost lost my pants." He laughs.

"Your turn." I point to Dad. "You said."

We climb the stairs together. Dad looks tired. He's a chef who works long hours on weekends. That's why we stay with him Sunday through Wednesday.

Dad stands aside. "You want to go first?"

"No, you go."

He lies back. "Like this?"

"Just like that."

He zips down the slide and flips over on his side as he hits the water. He sputters up coughing, and G-Man and Quinn laugh.

"Your turn, Jackson," Quinn shouts.

I lean back and make an X with my arms across my chest. I fly around the curves like I'm running around the bases. I whoosh underwater and swim to the surface.

G-Man says you have to challenge yourself. The traveling team, middle school, Snuffy's homework, going between Mom's and Dad's, finding a second baseman: I've got enough challenges.

CHAPTER 5

"You swing like an old lady." Gig's giving me a hard time about batting left-handed at recess.

"You try it, Big Mouth." I hand him the bat and lean against the metal fence. We'd all love to be able to switch-hit like Diego.

Gig pounds the bat on the plate as dust whips up. "I'm going to destroy the first good pitch I see."

Diego grooves one down the middle and Gig swings so hard he spins all the way around.

We all burst out laughing. "You destroyed it, all right," I say.

"Give me another one." Gig stands up. "I wasn't ready."

Diego throws and Gig swings and the aluminum bat goes flying. I duck to avoid it.

"What are you doing, Gig?" I holler. "You're going to kill somebody."

"You're making it harder than it is," Diego calls from the mound. "You both drop the bat too low when you swing. Keep the bat level, the same way you do from the right side." He demonstrates a smooth swing.

I dig in, but it still feels strange this way. Diego pitches and I tap a dribbler down the third-base line. I'm never going to be able to hit like him from this side.

"Let me try again." Gig grabs the bat. "I'll show you."

"Don't take somebody's head off this time, Gig," Isaac yells.

"Why are you called Gig anyway?" Diego rubs the ball.

"In first grade, our teacher said I was like a whirligig, something that's constantly moving." Gig shakes his hips and jumps around. "Whirligig's too long for a nickname, but Isaac started calling me Gig and it stuck."

"Batter up," I shout.

Diego grooves a pitch, and Gig swings so hard, he spins around and falls on his butt. We all crack up laughing, including Gig.

*I*n art class, Ms. Langley has a pile of stuff stacked on the floor, and kids swarm around it like it's pirate treasure.

"My favorite." Gig finds an empty Tostitos bag and licks his finger and rubs it inside for crumbs.

"What's all this junk for?" Trenton holds up rainbow wrapping paper and a plastic spoon.

"I'll explain." Ms. Langley smiles. "Everybody take a seat." She has short, black hair, a long neck, and likes to smile.

I sit next to Gig and look up at the art posters Ms. Langley has tacked to the ceiling. She lets us sit where we want and usually has something fun to do. Even though gym is my favorite class, Ms. Langley is my favorite teacher.

"We're going to make self-portraits using found objects." She waves at the pile. She's wearing purple glasses today to match her skirt. "I brought a bunch of material in, but I want you to bring in some treasures of your own next week." She grabs a box and sets it on our table. "Take one of these and pass it around."

I take out a small black mirror and open it.

"Take a good look at yourself," Ms. Langley says.

I concentrate on my green eyes and short brown hair. I try to ignore my ears that I wish were smaller. I squish up my lips and stick out my tongue.

Gig pulls the corners of eyes down and his mouth up while he looks at himself. He reaches out with his two little fingers and pushes up his nose. "Snnnn, snnnn," he sniffs. "'I see you boys have not finished your work,'" he says in his Snuffy voice. "'I'm disappointed. Very disappointed.'"

"Focus on the color of your skin," Ms. Langley says. "Each of you has a different skin tone. Today you're going to mix paint to try to match it."

I look at my face in the mirror. What color is it exactly? I set my hand on the white paper on my table. It's not white like that. Nobody's is. It's more light tan. And some parts of my hand, like the palm, are lighter than others.

"What about freckles?" Gig waves his hand.

"Freckles are on the skin," Ms. Langley says. "Pay attention to their color."

"What about zits?" Gig touches his cheek and some kids laugh.

"Those are optional." She smiles as she sets out paints, brushes, and cups.

I open up the paints and mix yellow and white on my palette. Art's a nice break from Snuffy.

"What else do you need to add, Jackson?" She looks over my shoulder. Ms. Langley never says she's disappointed in us.

I mix some brown in and hold my hand next to it. It's still

too light. I add a couple of drops of black and stir. Closer, but still not right. It's amazing all the colors I have to add to come close to my skin's.

After school, G-Man pulls into the parking lot of Diego's apartment building, and I search for him. None of my other friends live in apartments.

"Over there." I spot Diego waiting on the steps with his glove in his hand.

G-Man drives the Buick over and stops.

I open the back door. "Hey, Diego, this is G-Man."

"Hi, G-Man." Diego shakes his hand.

"Nice to meet you, Diego."

"Thanks for picking me up."

"No problem." G-Man steers the car out of the lot. "I hear you can hit and pitch. I'm eager to see you do both. *¿Hablas español?*" G-Man glances in the rearview mirror.

"*Sí.*"

"*¿De dónde eres tú?*"

"*San Antonio.*"

"*¿De dónde son tus padres?*"

"*Puebla.*"

"*¿La ciudad o el estado?*"

"*La ciudad.*"

"*Puebla es una ciudad bonita. ¡Me encanta mole poblano!*"

Diego smiles. "*Yo también.*"

"What in the world are you talking about?" I turn to Diego.

"Where my parents are from and what G-Man likes to eat."

"I've been telling you, Jackson. You have to learn Spanish." G-Man taps the steering wheel while he waits to turn at the light.

"I told you. It's not offered at Cranston. I'll take it next year at Longview."

G-Man nods. "*Muy bien.*"

"**S**pread out to stretch." Coach Wilkins, Isaac's dad, walks among us on the outfield grass. He's wearing black shorts, a red Suburban Athletic League polo shirt, and wraparound sunglasses.

I unwrap a piece of bubble gum and count. Eight players. Not even enough for a team.

"Put your right leg in front of you and cross your left over to set the foot flat on the ground next to the knee." Coach sits down and demonstrates.

"We've only got eight." I turn to Gig, who flips his leg over. He's as flexible as a wet noodle.

"Somebody might be late."

"Now turn to the left," Coach says.

I feel like a pretzel as I twist around.

"Okay, slowly come back and do the other side."

"I'm ready," Gig says. "Let's play ball."

"We're getting there. One last stretch. Both legs in front of you and bend at the waist."

I try that, but don't bend forward very far. I'm with Gig. Let's start the real practice.

Coach stands up and adjusts his sunglasses. "Okay, everybody, come over here."

We all crowd around him.

"We're going to have fun this year," he says. "That's the main goal, but we're also going to improve every game and become a good baseball team." He looks around at each of us. "We're going to work together and play the game right. We're short on numbers, so if you know someone who might want to play, encourage him to come out."

I draw a blank. I've already asked everybody I could think of.

"Run out to the position you want to play." Coach claps.

I run to short, the best position on the field. Gig races to the mound. Diego takes first and Tony Cerrato's at third. In the outfield, Isaac's in center, Steve Stein's in left, and Cole Gunderson's in right. Behind the plate, Noah Hauser is catching.

But nobody is at second.

As I blow a bubble, I hear a clatter on the hill behind first base. I turn to see a boy on a bike racing down. He pulls up to the fence and leans the bike down.

Then I realize it's not a boy. It's Gig's sister, Sydney. What happened? Why is she here?

She pulls a black glove out of her backpack. "I want to play."

I look at Gig on the mound. His mouth is open and his eyes are bugging out. Everybody else, including Coach, is staring at Sydney as she walks onto the field.

Who does she think she is?

CHAPTER 6

"**W**hat are you doing?" Gig shouts.

"I'm here to play second." Sydney smacks her glove. "You need a second baseman. I play second. It works."

"No, it doesn't." Gig's face is red as he walks toward her. "You don't belong here. You play *softball*, not baseball."

"You know, I've always liked baseball better. Baseball's my favorite sport, not softball." She looks calmly at him. "I talked with Mr. Eberhart, the commissioner of the Suburban Athletic League. He said if a sport is not available for girls, girls can play on the boys' team. So here I am."

"No way, Squid Face!" Gig's bouncing back and forth and looks like he's about to punch her.

"That's enough, Gig." Coach steps between them. "Sydney, it would have been helpful to know in advance you were coming."

"I'm sorry, Coach Wilkins. Mr. Eberhart only told me fifteen minutes ago. I rushed right over because Jackson said you needed someone." Sydney looks at him coolly like it's the most natural thing in the world for her to show up at our practice.

She shouldn't have brought me into it. Gig paces around like he's going to explode.

"We need to work this out." Coach takes off his sunglasses and rubs his eyes.

"There's nothing to work out," Gig shouts. "She should leave us alone."

Coach picks up a bat. If he lets Sydney play, Gig's going to be furious. If he tells her she can't, she'll go straight to Mr. Eberhart, and we'll get in trouble for not following the rules. We might have to forfeit all of our games.

"Infielders, get ready for some ground balls." Coach walks to the plate. "Sydney, give it a try at second base."

She jogs out to second base, and Gig kicks at the pitcher's mound.

Coach ignores him and hits a two-hopper to me at short. I scoop it up and throw to Diego. The throw is low, but Diego digs it out of the dirt.

"Good pick, Diego," Coach calls. "Sydney, are you ready?"

"Yes, Coach Wilkins." She bends down in her stance.

He hits a grounder toward second and she moves to her right. She tries to backhand the ball, but it hits the heel of her glove and skips into centerfield. Isaac jogs in to pick it up and throws to Noah, the catcher, who hands it to Coach.

"See, I told you," Gig says. "She doesn't belong here."

"Try it again, Sydney." Coach hits a bouncer to her left and Sydney slides over. She puts her glove down, but the ball squirts under for another error.

"It's this new glove." Sydney takes it off and holds it up. "I'm not used to it. Let me get my regular glove." She runs to her pack and pulls out another one—a bright pink glove.

"That's not a baseball glove." Gig looks like he's going to die of humiliation as Diego and Noah laugh.

Sydney races back to second. "Let me try again. This is my lucky glove."

I pick a clod of mud off my cleats. A pink glove! I can't believe she's doing this to Gig. To us.

Coach hits a two-hopper, and she grabs it cleanly and throws to Diego. Coach rubs his chin while she gets in position. He smacks a sizzler toward the bag. Sydney moves right, reaches out, and snags it. She turns and throws to first.

That was a good stop. Not just for a girl. For anybody.

"Nice grab," Coach says.

Gig takes off his glove and whips it against the fence.

"Take it easy, Gig," Coach says. "Control yourself."

I flex my hand. I've seen Gig angry plenty of times. But never like this.

After practice, Isaac, Gig, Diego, and I sit on the bench. Isaac pulls out water bottles from a cooler and passes them around.

"I'm thirstier than a dehydrated camel." I take a huge drink.

"Two dehydrated camels," Diego says as we all watch Sydney climb on her bike.

"See you tomorrow, Coach Wilkins." She waves.

"Good work, Sydney," he calls.

"She got better after she switched gloves," Isaac says. "She might be okay."

"She's not okay." Gig spits water on the ground. "Believe me, Barf Breath's a disaster. She thinks she's smarter than anyone else. She'll start telling all of us what to do. She'll try to run the team."

"We need a second baseman," I say. "She's better than nothing. Even with that goofy glove."

"No, she's not," Gig says. "She's worse. *Way* worse. She'll ruin everything." He drains his water in a big gulp.

"What can we do?" I squeeze the cap of the bottle in my hand. I never should have told Sydney we needed a second baseman.

"Make her quit." Gig throws his water bottle at the trash can, and it hits the side and bounces off. "Make it so she won't want to be on our team." He gets up and walks to his bike.

"Gig, wait." I chase after him. "Do you want to come over tonight? I'll ask my mom." I stand in front of him.

"No." He pulls away. "I want to be alone."

"See you tomorrow then."

"Jackson"—he turns as he rides away—"do what you can to force her out."

CHAPTER 7

At school Tuesday, Diego's carrying a big box from Wollum's Bakery.

"What's that?" I peak inside. Black cupcakes with black sprinkles are lined up in rows. "Can I have one?"

"No, they're for my class. I'm eleven today."

"Happy birthday." A cupcake would taste really good. "Are you having a party?"

"I had a family party on Sunday."

"Are you having a friend party, too?"

"No, just the family one."

Diego's eleven now and so is Isaac. Because he was held back a year, Gig's twelve. I'm the only one who's stuck on ten. I can't help it that my birthday's in June, but I feel like I'm way behind everybody else.

Kids push against one another as they hang jackets in their lockers. "Give me some space," Gig yells.

He looks like he's still mad about Sydney. "Hey, it's going to be okay." I walk over to him.

"It is not." He turns to me and glares.

"I was just trying to help."

"You don't know what it's like having her for a sister." He shakes his head. "Teachers always ask me why can't you be more like Sydney. But I'm *not* her, and I don't want to be like her."

"I don't want you to be like her, either."

"Baseball was the one place I didn't have to deal with her. Now she wants to wreck that, too."

I don't know what to say or do, so I stand there like an idiot. Gig looks like he's about to cry.

"Is anything else bugging you?"

He nods.

"What?"

He turns away. "Dad."

"What?"

"Dad's unit is being called up."

"Why?" Gig's dad is in the National Guard and last year

they packed sandbags to protect homes from flooding in the spring. He was on TV and everything.

"He told us at breakfast. He has to go to Mississippi for six weeks of training. Then he's going to Afghanistan. For the war."

I should say something, but I don't know what.

"He's going to be gone for a year."

I can't imagine not seeing my dad for a year.

"If everything goes okay." Gig slumps against his locker.

*D*uring math, Mrs. Spanier explains percentages, but I can't concentrate. I watch Gig stare out the window. I can't remember seeing him like this.

"What is ten percent of twenty, Jackson?"

"What?"

"Ten percent of twenty?" Mrs. Spanier holds out her hands like I'm supposed to give her something.

"I don't know."

"What about you, Spencer?"

"What?"

"I asked you a simple question. What is ten percent of twenty?"

"I don't know."

"Pay attention." Mrs. Spanier raises her voice. "You boys act like your minds are elsewhere."

I rub my nose and sniff to try to get Gig to laugh, but he's not paying any attention. Of course, our minds are elsewhere.

"On Friday, we have our middle school visits. You will visit either Eagle Bluff or Longview, depending on where you are going next year," Mrs. Spanier says. "Remember, you never get a second chance to make a good first impression. It is extremely important that you do so. I expect everybody to be on his or her best behavior." She looks at Gig and then me. "The way some of you are acting, you're not ready for middle school. You could use another year in fifth grade."

Another year with Snuffy—that would be cruel and unusual punishment.

CHAPTER

"**I**'m so sick of Snuffy's homework." At lunch, Gig grabs his stomach and pretends to puke.

"Please." Isaac cuts into his cheese omelet. "We're eating."

"Snuffy called my mom again to say I'm missing assignments," Gig complains. "I wouldn't be behind if she didn't give us so much work. Of course my mom and dad took the teacher's side."

"Parents always do." I spread butter on my cinnamon roll. "They don't understand how hard school is."

"They think our homework is easy." Gig talks with his mouth full. "It's easy for them because they've already had it. We haven't learned it yet. That's why it's homework."

"Yeah," Diego jumps in. "If I'm trying my best and get a bad grade, my parents say I'm not trying. Even when I am."

Isaac finishes his orange juice. "My parents expect me to be perfect, but then they say have fun. They don't realize that it's impossible to do both."

"We're fifth graders. We need to have fun." I hand my orange slices to Gig.

"Thanks." He jams one in his mouth to make an orange wedge smile. "It's stinkin' hard work to be a fifth grader," he mutters through the fruit.

"It is." I bite into my cinnamon roll. "This is the best lunch."

"I agree." Diego wipes frosting from his mouth.

"Italian dunkers is," Isaac says.

"Mini corn dogs." Gig taps the table. "They fit perfectly up your nose."

I'm glad to see him joking around again. Did he tell any of the other guys about his dad going to Afghanistan? I finish my chocolate milk and crumple the carton. If he didn't, should I?

Gig swings at a pitch from Coach Wilkins and bounces a grounder up the middle. Sydney moves to her right, stabs it with her pink glove, and throws to Diego.

Coach whistles. "Nice play, Sydney."

Gig pounds his bat on the ground. He hasn't hit anything out of the infield. He's not playing like usual. I'm not crazy about Sydney being here either, but what are we supposed to do? We only have eight players without her. If we don't have nine, we'd have to forfeit.

"Keep your head down, Gig," Coach says. "You're pulling your head up early." He throws a pitch down the middle.

Gig swings wildly and misses. It's not his day.

"Diego, you're up." Coach picks up balls by the mound. "Gig, take first."

Diego runs in and puts on a batting helmet. He grabs the red bat and digs in at the plate. He rips the first pitch into the gap between right and center. I can't believe we had to persuade him to come out. He lines four more shots to the outfield before he switches and bats from the left side.

He knocks the first pitch from that side on a scorching one-hopper to second. Sydney goes down to one knee, sticks out her glove, and makes a clean grab. She throws to Gig at first.

"Great stab," Coach shouts.

Gig stands at first and waits to throw the ball to Coach. He won't look at Sydney, and I try not to, either. She's decent in the field—a lot better than I thought.

Diego laces the next pitch off the fence in center field.

"Three more feet and that was out of here." Isaac races to retrieve the ball.

"You're up, Sydney," Coach calls. "Gig, take second. Diego, back to first."

Sydney hustles in and selects the smallest batting helmet. She adjusts it on her head and looks over the bats. She picks the silver one, the lightest one, and takes a couple of practice swings. She steps into the batter's box and straightens her helmet.

"Everybody ready?" Coach calls. He throws the first pitch and Sydney swings and misses.

"Strike one," Gig calls out.

"Relax up there." Coach winds up and throws.

Sydney hits a slow roller that hugs the first-base line. Diego barehands it and flips to Coach.

Sydney raises her hand for time and digs in with her back foot.

"All set?" Coach delivers.

Sydney swings and hits a bouncer toward second. I run to my left and lunge, but I can't reach it. Gig dives and comes up with a glove full of dirt.

"Base hit," Coach says. "That's the way."

I lean down beside Gig, who's sprawled on the outfield grass. He's frowning and looks like he's been punched in the gut.

"I can't handle it." He shakes his head. "I can't stand having Squid Face on our team. She's wrecking everything."

"She's not that bad." I offer him a hand.

"Yes, she is." He refuses my hand and pushes himself up. "You've got to choose, Jackson. Me or her."

"You know I'm with you." I walk back to short. It's hard watching him get all twisted up about Sydney. Of course I'm with him. We're best friends.

CHAPTER 9

When Dad picks me up after practice, Quinn is bouncing up and down in the backseat. "We're going to the Orange Octopus to get the Subaru washed."

I climb in front.

"It won't take long." Dad hands me a Gatorade and a tangerine. "I promised Quinn a car wash, and then we'll grab a bite to eat."

I take off my hat and hold the cold plastic bottle against my sweaty forehead.

"How was practice?" Dad looks over at me.

"Good." I don't feel like talking about Gig and Sydney. She might still quit on her own. Maybe she's not really serious. Maybe she's just messing with Gig.

"How much longer?" Quinn's searching for signs.

"Keep watching," Dad says.

"G-Man keeps trying to get me to go out for the traveling team this year." I twist off the cap and take a drink.

"You seemed clear about your choice." Dad brakes for a light.

"Yeah, but it's not what he wants."

"It's not his decision," Dad says. "You have to know what you want. Otherwise, he'll decide for you." He scratches his neck. "I remember when I quit baseball senior year to take a job as a busboy at the country club. My dad told me it was a mistake I'd regret the rest of my life, but I don't regret it at all. He didn't like it when I went to culinary school, rather than college either, but he came around. He'll push, but if you stand your ground with him, he'll respect your decision."

"I wonder if he'll still go to the park with me this weekend to hit grounders."

"Ask him. He likes to be asked."

"Look." Quinn spies the sign of the orange octopus holding sponges, soap, and brushes. "We're here."

It's a lot easier being six when something as simple as a car wash is a big deal. Dad takes out his wallet, selects the wash, and swipes his credit card.

"Gig got some bad news today." I set the bottle in the cup holder.

"What?" Dad turns to me.

"His dad has to go to Afghanistan with the National Guard."

"When?" Dad rubs his chin like he does when he's thinking.

"I'm not sure." I roll the tangerine around in my palm like it's a baseball.

"Where's Afghanistan?" Quinn asks.

"In Asia," Dad says. "Next to Pakistan."

"And Iran. We learned that in social studies." I unpeel the skin.

"That's right." Dad drives in and the door closes behind us. "Let Gig know we'll do anything we can to help." Dad turns off the engine and soap sprays while the brushes beat against the car.

When I get on the bus on Wednesday, Gig's not in our usual seat in back. He's not on the bus anywhere. I slide in next to Noah Hauser, the catcher. "Where's Gig?"

"He didn't get on this morning when his sister did." He points up front where Sydney's talking with Kelsey Neeley.

Is Gig staying home in protest? Is he mad I didn't get Sydney to quit?

"It's going to be hot this afternoon." Hauser wipes a sleeve across his forehead. "I'm going to die with all that catcher's gear on."

"Yeah." I stare out the window. I'm glad I get to play short where I just have to put on my hat and glove. I watch the houses go by—the same ones I see every day on the way to school—and think about Gig. As his best friend, I have to talk with Sydney.

I follow Sydney as we walk into school. She's wearing capris and a yellow flowing top, and she and Kelsey say hi to everyone.

"Good morning, Jackson." Principal Maroney waves.

"Good morning," I say, even though it's not.

When Kelsey turns off for her classroom, I have my chance. "Sydney."

"Yes." She turns to me and smiles.

"It's about the team." It's hard to look at her directly and say what I want, so I look at the D.A.R.E. bulletin board over her shoulder.

"The team's great, and Coach Wilkins is such a good coach. I'm really glad to be on the Panthers."

"That's what I want to talk with you about." I move closer,

but keep looking past her. "You're good enough to play with us. It's not that. But it would be better if you didn't."

"What are you talking about?" She puts her hands on her hips and leans forward.

"You know what it will be like. Guys on other teams will give us a hard time if we have a girl."

"So what. You can take it."

"They'll give you a hard time, too, especially if you use that pink glove."

"I can handle that. I'm going to play baseball."

Gig's right. She is stubborn. "Sydney, Gig doesn't want you on the team. Think about him. Think what you're doing to him."

"I'm not doing it to him." She shakes her head. "I'm doing it for me."

"But he's having a hard time with your dad going and everything."

"What makes you think it's easy for me, Jackson?" Her brown eyes narrow and lock on to mine. "I'm having a hard time, too." She looks down. "When I was little, I played catch with my dad. Baseball, not softball. He says it's fine for me to play, and it helps take my mind off him leaving."

That shuts me up and I turn to walk to my classroom. Of course it makes sense that Sydney is scared about her dad leaving. I just don't picture her struggling with anything.

Talking to her was supposed to help, but I'm more confused than ever.

CHAPTER 10

"**S**ydney shouldn't play with us." Diego digs into his nachos at lunch.

"Why not?" Isaac asks.

"Because it's a boys' team," Diego says. "She can play softball."

"And because Gig doesn't want her to." I wipe some cheese from my chin. "He was on the team first. She didn't even ask him about it."

"Yeah, but we need someone at second." Isaac spoons up some nasty-looking peaches.

"We've got two days until our first game. We can still find someone else." I lick my finger.

"Like who?" Isaac says. "We tried. We couldn't get anyone else."

"I'm trying to bribe Trenton." I scoop up some hamburger that's fallen off my nachos.

"He won't do it," Isaac says.

"Maybe we should ignore Sydney," Diego says.

"That won't work," I say. "She's really stubborn."

"Maybe you could persuade her to quit." Diego sips his chocolate milk.

I shake my head. "I tried that. She's not quitting."

"Well, find somebody new then," Isaac says.

"I'm trying. I'm trying." I tear open the sticky wrapper on my ice cream bar. Why am I responsible for everything?

"Friday's the day for middle school visits," Isaac says. "Gig won't miss that."

"My brother said to watch out for eighth graders," Diego says. "He said if you get separated from the group, you're asking for trouble."

"How is that asking for trouble?" I bite into my ice cream bar. Too bad Gig's not here. These are his favorites.

"Just don't get separated," Diego warns.

"They have huge fights in middle school," Isaac says.

"Yeah, sometimes the bullies fight each other, but most of the time they pick on sixth graders," Diego says. "My brother said to be careful of eighth graders putting stuff in your backpack. Sometimes they hide drugs and then you get busted."

"Why would they do that?" I shake my head.

"To get you in trouble," Diego says.

We sit quietly for a minute and finish our lunches. Fights, bullies, drugs—middle school is going to be way different from fifth grade. We'll go from being the biggest kids in the school to the smallest. And every eighth-grade bully will be waiting to beat us up. We've got to stick together. Then I remember that Isaac is going to Eagle Bluff on his school visit, not Longview. He's going to be on his own. At least I'll have Gig and Diego with me. I wouldn't go off to middle school without friends for all the money in the world.

"I read a message this morning from another fifth grader worried about middle school," Isaac says. "At a Web site called FutureMe where you can send a message to yourself in the future."

"What do you mean?" I crumple my ice-cream wrapper into a little ball and stuff it into the plastic peach cup.

"You write an e-mail to yourself that will be delivered in the future. It can be six months, a year, ten years, whenever you want."

"Why would anybody do that?" Diego asks.

"I don't know," Isaac says. "If you predicted something, you could see if it came true. If you set a goal, you could send yourself a reminder to see if you'd reached it."

"Sounds dumb," Diego says.

I push my tray away. "What's the Web site?"

"FutureMe-dot-org," Isaac says. "It doesn't have pictures or video or anything, but you can read other people's messages. Some are really funny."

During writing time, Mrs. Spanier hands back our papers. "I'm disappointed in your work. Very disappointed." She shakes her head like we're the worst class she's ever had. "You were supposed to write a description of snow for someone who's never seen snow before. That was a question last year on the statewide tests. You're supposed to have an introduction, three examples, and a conclusion. Some of you only had two examples, some of you had no conclusion, and one of you said to come visit me in January and see for yourself."

I catch a glimpse of the paper she's looking at while kids laugh. It's Gig's.

"I'm serious. This test is very important. You are ranked on this. I am ranked on this. The school district is ranked on this. It is of utmost importance that you take this test seriously and do well on it."

I look at Gig's empty desk. I wonder what he's doing now. The day feels like it's lasted forever without him.

"Some of you are doing a very poor job with spelling, punctuation, and grammar." Mrs. Spanier sniffs. "We expect more from fifth graders. If you want to be ready for middle school, you need to pay more attention to your writing."

Mrs. Spanier hands me my paper that's so marked up in red it looks like a squirrel bled to death on it. Such a stupid topic. Someone who's never seen snow could just watch a movie. They wouldn't need to read a paper about it.

"Next week we'll have a special treat," Mrs. Spanier says. "Mr. Selby, who is a local writer, is coming in from the Writers in the Schools program. He's going to help you with your writing, and judging from these papers, many of you need a lot of help."

Working on writing isn't a treat. Only a teacher would say that. If I'm getting a treat, I'd much rather have a Krispy Kreme doughnut.

———

On the way home, I get off at Gig's stop. I don't have to worry about Sydney because she stayed after school with the other suck-ups to make posters with Mrs. Spanier for National Electrical Safety Month.

I walk up the driveway to the townhouse, climb the cement steps, and push the doorbell. Nobody answers, but I know he's here. I press again.

"Hi, Jackson." Mrs. Milroy's eyes are red as she opens the door.

"Is Gig home?"

"Yes. He's not feeling well, though."

"Can I talk to him for just a minute. It's important."

"I guess so if you're not worried about catching his germs." She leads me in.

I climb the stairs and see Gig's dad at the kitchen table smoking a cigar. "Hi, Mr. Milroy."

"Hi, Jackson." He tries to smile, but the lines on his face make him look sad.

I should probably say something about him going to Afghanistan, but I don't know what. Nothing that pops in my head, like "I'm sorry" or "That's too bad," sounds right. I walk to Gig's room and knock on his door.

"Yeah," he answers in a bored voice.

I talk lower to disguise my voice. "I've never seen snow and would like to come to your house in January." I open the door.

"Very funny," he says.

"What's up?" I pull a mountain of clothes off a chair and sit down.

"Nothing. I don't feel good." He looks up from his video game.

"What's the matter?" He looks pale.

"My stomach hurts."

"Are you coming to practice?"

"No."

"Because you're sick or because of Sydney?"

"Because I'm sick of Sydney."

I lean back on the couch. "I've got good news. I found a second baseman for us. Someone to replace Sydney."

"Who?" His eyes widen.

"Trenton Casey."

"He's no good."

"He's a boy. He can play second. That's what you wanted. C'mon, Gig. We need you. You're our best pitcher. You're our most valuable player."

"Squid Face talked to Mom and Dad," he says quietly. "They took her side. They always do."

"But Isaac and Diego and I are all on your side."

"She always convinces them that she's right and then they expect me to agree." Gig rubs his stomach. "You better go. I feel like I'm gonna blow."

CHAPTER 11

I type www.FutureMe.org and open the site that Isaac was talking about. It's a basic site with the option to send your own message or to view other people's. I click on View Public Entries and read a message labeled "Get to Work."

Hey, you,

Are you still wasting time? Get to work.

Are you still doing all your studying at the last minute? Get to work.

Are you still clicking around the Internet to find pictures of naked girls? Get to work.

I'm giving you some directions and I want you to follow them exactly.

If you do so, you can achieve your dream of being an orthodontist.

If you don't, you will be a loser for life.

1. Get up every day at 7:00 and exercise.

2. Pay attention in all your classes.

3. Don't hang around with screw-offs.

4. Do all of your homework right when you get home from school.

5. No TV, video games, or movies until homework is finished.

6. Do all extra credit. You need it!

7. Don't eat junk food. Especially Twinkies.

8. Don't stay up late watching TV, talking on the phone, or texting.

If you do not follow these directions, you will not be an orthodontist.

You will let down:

1. Dad

2. Mom

3. Grandma

4. Grandpa

5. Mrs. Knoppler

6. Dr. Bob and all the orthodontists who have
   encouraged you
7. Yourself

Are you still wasting time? Get to Work.
Forrest

Hey, Forrest, relax. Take it easy. Even if you become an orthodontist, I wouldn't want you poking around in my mouth
if you're going to be so extreme.

I click on "random" to see another message.

Sarah,
   I hope you haven't sold out your beliefs for a nice
house and a pile of cash.
   You better not have or I'll come into the future and
beat you up.
   Remember me.

I click again.

Hey Dave,
   Are you still smoking?
   How many hundreds of times have you promised to quit?

Put down the cancer sticks right now. You owe it to
Riley and Samantha. They need to have their daddy
around. Quit. Right now.

J Dog,
   The world didn't blow up, did it? You worried for no
reason. Since you're reading this, you're still alive, too.
Congratulations on making it through your teenage
years.

I keep reading messages. Some are in foreign languages,
but most are in English. Some of the messages have already
been received by the future self, but others won't be received
for ten or twenty years. Will people have the same e-mail
address for that long?

It is a cool idea, though. What would I tell my future self?

"*I* told you I'd find somebody." I point to Trenton, who's
pedaling down the hill on his mountain bike. "He wants to
play second base for us."

"How'd you do that?" Isaac asks. "He already said no."

"It cost me." I pull on my glove. "Two old Spider-Mans
and an Amazing Hulk."

In the dugout, Sydney puts her hair in a ponytail and pulls it out the back of her hat. "Hi, Jackson," she says.

I turn away. She's got no clue she's about to lose her position.

"Welcome, Trenton." Coach Wilkins extends his hand. "What position do you play?"

Trenton looks to me and I mouth it.

"Second base," he says.

Sydney stares at him and then at me. I turn away and quickly run onto the field.

"Let's see what you can do," Coach says. "Go out there with Sydney. Everybody, let's take some infield practice."

It's a clear day with only a couple clouds in the sky. I've found a new second baseman. I've solved our problem. That should make Gig feel better fast.

"Here you go, Jackson." Coach hits a sharp grounder. I field it on the third hop and throw to Diego.

"Nice pick," he hollers.

"Sydney, you're up." Coach hits a bouncer that she grabs and throws to Diego. He doesn't say anything to her, and I don't, either.

"Okay, Trenton." Coach points the bat at him.

Trenton crouches in his stance and gets ready. He shuffles

forward and reaches with his glove, but the ball skips underneath into the outfield.

"You can do it," I say.

"Try again." Coach hits a ground-hugger toward second base.

Trenton moves to his right, but when he sticks his hand down, the ball hits the side of his glove and rolls off.

I walk over. "I thought you said you could play."

"I haven't played in a long time. I'm rusty."

"We're just finding out what you can do," Coach says. "Take one more." He hits a slow roller that Trenton charges. He bends down to pick it up, but his feet get tangled up, and he falls over on his butt.

"I thought I had it." He examines his glove.

Diego shakes his head.

"Let's try you in right field," Coach says. "We always need extra outfielders."

I kick at the dirt behind second base. Two Spider-Mans and an Amazing Hulk down the drain. I look over at Sydney, who flashes an ear-to-ear grin.

Later, we practice double plays. Coach hits a fast hopper to me and I throw the ball to Sydney. She steps on the base and turns to first and fires to Diego.

"Nice play," I say and then catch myself. I'm not supposed to say anything to encourage her.

Coach hits a shot to second that she backhands and flips to me. I grab it going across the bag and throw it to Diego.

"Good work out there," Coach hollers. "You're looking sharp."

I jog back to short. Sydney can play second. Trenton can't. That's the worst news in the world for Gig. For us.

"That's a tall tower." I get down on the floor to play Matchbox cars with Quinn, who's built another elaborate city out of blocks in the dining room at Dad's house.

"It's an insurance building," he says.

How many other six-year-olds do you know who build insurance buildings out of blocks?

"If you drive, you have to have insurance," Quinn says.

"That's right." I steer a Corvette over a bridge and around the leg of the table. "What's that?" I point to a fenced-in area with three cars in front.

"The dog park," Quinn says. "That's where dogs can run without a leash."

My phone rings in my backpack and I rush to get it. "Hello."

"Jackson, it's me," Mom says, which is totally unnecessary.

I know it's her. "I just talked to Ted. He wants to take us all out for a special dinner at the White Horse on Friday. Don't schedule anything."

"Mom, I've got a game on Friday. Our first game of the season."

"Oh, that's right. How could I forget that?"

I rub my forehead. I don't know how she could forget something so important.

"I'm sorry, Jackson. Ted and the girls have a wedding on Saturday. That's why we picked Friday." She pauses. "I know. Why don't we all come to your game and then go out?"

"No," I say quickly. "I don't want everybody at my game. I'll meet you afterward."

"What time?"

"Around eight."

"That will work. Meet us at the restaurant as soon as you can. It will really be fun. You and Quinn will like Heather and Haley. They're lovely girls."

I don't say anything.

"See you after school tomorrow."

"'Bye." I snap the phone shut.

"Everything okay?" Dad looks in from the kitchen.

"Yeah," I lie. Between Gig and Sydney and Mom and Ted, I've got too much going on, but I don't want to talk about any of it. I feel like that guy Gig told us about—the one who burst his brain.

CHAPTER 12

In gym class, I sit next to Gig. "How's your stomach?"

"Not great." He examines the floor. "Dad leaves for training in ten weeks."

"Sorry." I'm probably the only one who knows. I didn't tell the other guys. I thought Gig should if he wanted them to know. "My dad said we'd do anything to help. Just let me know."

"There's one thing you can do."

"What? Anything." I look at him, but his eyes dart around.

"One huge thing."

"What?"

"Get Squid Face off the team."

"I'm trying, Gig. I'm trying. Talking to her. Not talking to her. Bribing Trenton to come out. I'm trying everything. Nothing's working."

"Try harder."

Mr. Kahn lines up balls in the middle of the gym. "Count off by fours."

I slide one place over so Gig and I will be on the same team. "One," I shout.

"Two," Hauser calls.

"Three," Gig says.

Mr. Kahn watches everybody count off. He's strict, but he lets us play all kinds of games, even dodgeball, which Mrs. Spanier says is too dangerous for school.

"Split into two teams," Mr. Kahn calls. "Ones and fours together down here. Twos and threes together down there."

"Dang," I say. He crossed us up. Gig shrugs his shoulders, and I jog down to the other end.

"Ready, set, go," Mr. Kahn shouts.

I race to the middle and grab a green ball. I retreat quickly to the corner and find Gig. He's their hardest thrower and it's important to know where he is.

Balls fly and lots of kids get hit and go out. I always wait a bit for the initial chaos to die down. Too many kids race to the front and go out right away.

A lazy throw drifts toward me and I drop the green ball to

catch it. "You're out," I holler, though I don't know who threw it.

A ball slams against the wall beside my head. I turn to see Gig standing at the half-court line. I race up and throw at his feet. He jumps over the ball. "Is that all you got?" He laughs.

At least he's smiling again. I retreat under the basket and we're already down to four on our team. I carefully move over to the corner. It's easier to see what's coming from over here. A red ball floats toward me and I reach to catch it. At the last moment, I spot another ball speeding for my head and duck. That's Gig.

"No balls to the head," Mr. Kahn says. "Bring them down below the chest."

When Gig throws at somebody else, I race to the line and hurl the ball at his body. He falls flat on the floor and the ball sails over the top. He hops up, grabs a ball, and nails another one of my teammates.

Only Kelsey and me are left against Gig and three others. Trenton is collecting balls and handing them to Gig, who's throwing hard.

"Go, Kelsey. Go, Jackson," a teammate hollers from the side.

"Finish them off, Gig," someone else yells.

Kelsey bends down to pick up a ball and Gig nails her in the butt. The ball bounces off and hits the rim of the basketball hoop, and everybody laughs.

Four against me, and Gig's throwing like he's possessed. I retreat to the wall and balls bang off as I duck and dodge. I don't even have time to bend down to pick up a ball as I keep my eyes on what's flying at me.

A purple one comes in and I grab it.

"Go, Jackson." My team cheers wildly.

Gig unleashes a wicked ball that I duck to avoid at the last second. I race up to the line to throw at him. A ball flies in from the side that I skip over. I turn to unload on Hauser. I hit him in the thigh and retreat to the wall. I keep an eye on Gig the whole time.

He whistles another one and I duck. He's throwing so hard that the balls are bouncing off the wall all the way back to him at half-court, and I'm pinned against the wall.

Trenton throws one; I turn to grab it. He leaves the floor to loud cheers.

Just Gig and me. One on one.

He fires a purple ball with all his might and I leap out of the way. Gig always goes all out, but I've never seen him throw harder. I sling a low one at his feet and he hops out of the way.

My only chance in this showdown is for him to get tired and for me to catch one of his throws. He blazes two more at me, and I move out of the way. He's not showing any signs of letting up.

"Hang in there, Jackson."

"Go, Gig. Wipe him out." Classmates yell and cheer on each throw.

Gig winds up and throws a red ball at me. Here's my chance. I reach to catch it and the ball thumps against my chest. I try to squeeze it, but the ball bounces up and out. I dive, but the ball hits the floor, and everybody on Gig's team cheers. They rush to congratulate him while I lie on the floor.

When I get home from school, I check out some more messages at FutureMe.org. A girl apologizes to a fourth-grade classmate she teased every day and says she doesn't know why she did it. A guy asks his future self if he's got a girlfriend yet and if he's kissed her. Another guy accuses his future self of forgetting about his past self and says this link between them is like a tightrope and he's afraid he's falling off.

I click on Create New Entry and start typing. I'm going to

send a message to my future self in a week. I type out the whole thing, even going back to fix my mistakes.

Hey FutureMe,

How's the team? What's going on between Gig and Sydney? Are they talking? Ignoring each other?

How are you doing at shortstop? Any errors? Remember, it's the best position on the field and you get to play it this year.

Are you making them throw strikes to you and not chasing bad pitches? Are you making every at-bat count?

You can beat any team in the league. Don't be intimidated by anyone.

Go, Panthers!

Your past self

When I press "Send this to the future," I get a message: "You must send your e-mail at least ninety days into the future."

Shoot. They should tell you that before you start typing. I've done all that work and want to send the message. What else can I do? Snail mail. I print out the message and go upstairs to Mom's desk to find an envelope.

I find one in the bottom drawer, fold my message, and lick the envelope closed. I address it to myself and search through drawers for a stamp. I can't find one anyplace. I'll have to ask Mom to pick one up for me next time she goes to the post office. That's why people don't use snail mail anymore. It's too much work.

"**A** couple more double plays." Coach Wilkins whacks a grounder at me at practice.

I take two steps to the left, field it cleanly, and toss to second. Sydney catches it and throws to first.

"Turn one." Coach hits a shot up the middle. Sydney dives and reaches with her pink glove to make the stop. She flips a throw to me from the ground. I relay quickly to Diego at first.

"Nice stop," I say as I retreat to short.

Gig glares at me from the mound.

Well, it was a nice stop. If she wasn't his sister, he'd say so, too. And if she wasn't his sister, he'd be glad to have her playing second base on our team. She's a good fielder. She makes the team better. She can't help it that she's related to him.

Chapter 13

*F*riday afternoon, when we pull into the parking lot of Longview Middle School, the building looks ginormous. How am I going to find my way to my classes next year without getting lost?

"Make sure you stay with your group," Mrs. Spanier says.

"Where else would we go?" Gig mutters under his breath, as he, Diego, and I stand up.

"Isaac should be with us." I smooth out my Adidas shirt.

"He could be here if he didn't have to go to stuck-up Chickadee Bluff." Gig rubs his hand through his hair to flatten it out. He's wearing cargo pants and his favorite T-shirt, the one with an arrow that says I'M WITH STUPID.

My stomach is feeling weird. Maybe I've got what Gig had. Maybe I ate my cheesy stuffed-crust pizza too fast at lunch. Or maybe I've got a severe case of middleschoolphobia.

"Welcome, students," a big guy with a thin mustache greets us. "I'm Assistant Principal Norquist, and I handle discipline here at Longview. I hope I don't see you much next year."

He doesn't look like anyone you'd want to see.

"Nice shoes," Gig says under his breath.

Norquist is wearing penny loafers that clash with his tough-guy pose.

"We have high expectations at Longview." Norquist goes into the same kind of speech that Snuffy's given us a hundred times about above-the-line behavior and what it takes to succeed. At the end he asks if there are any questions.

Sydney raises her hand and Mr. Norquist calls on her. Gig lowers his head in his hands.

"Mr. Norquist, how many books can we check out of the school library at one time?"

"That's the type of question we like." Mr. Norquist smiles. "What's your name?"

"Sydney Milroy."

"I think it's two, Sydney, but Mr. Amodt, the librarian, has some special book groups, and if you're in one of those, you can check out as many as you want."

"I want to sign up for that," Sydney says.

Gig leans over to me. "Do you see why she makes me sick?"

I keep watching for eighth graders, but they all seem to be in class. They probably plan it that way so we don't die of a heart attack on our first day.

Norquist shows us the gym, the auditorium, and the pool. "We've heard that you are the smartest group of new students we've ever had at Longview. We're expecting great things from you."

"I bet he says that every year," Gig whispers to me.

"We expect all of you to have a positive Longview attitude." Norquist sniffs.

"He sounds like Snuffy." I put my hand in front of my mouth.

"He sniffs like her, too," Gig says. "Maybe they're cousins."

All of a sudden, my stomach's gurgling in that way that means I have to get to a bathroom immediately. I see a sign for BOYS and rush to a stall. This shouldn't take long.

But it does. Once I start going, I can't stop, and it feels like everything I've eaten for the past couple of days wants to come out. I shake my head to clear my mind but still feel weird. It smells horrible. I wash my hands twice and rush into the hall. Everybody is gone. I don't see any of them.

I hurry past the art room and come to a corner. Left, right, or straight? I don't hear Mr. Norquist or anybody from the group. I turn right and head down the hall. After all the warnings about staying with the group, I'm by myself in the halls of Longview Middle School.

Another decision. I turn right. Another corner. Now I feel like I'm walking around in a giant square. Ahead a couple of guys big enough to play in the NFL are opening their lockers. I turn around and walk fast in the other direction before they see me. I pass a tall girl with short brown hair who looks like a supermodel. She seems about ten years older than the girls in our class.

Down a dark hall, something white appears at the end. I walk toward it. It can't be. A beautiful girl with long blond hair and a flowing white dress hovers two feet off the ground. I stop and stare. She slowly lifts up her hand, looks straight at me, and beckons to me to come forward.

I turn around and run as fast as I can. Down one hall and then another.

Finally I stumble into the library. "I need help," I tell the man at the desk. "I'm here with a group from Cranston Elementary School and I got separated from them."

"That's not a good way to start." He shakes his head and

looks up over his glasses. He's got curly black hair, thick side-burns, and muscleman arms. "What's your name?"

"Jackson Kennedy."

He calls the office and finds out where my group is and points to a chair. "Sit down, Jackson. Someone will come and get you. We don't need you wandering these halls alone when you don't know your way around."

I nod in agreement. I sure don't want to be wandering around with ghosts.

"I'm Mr. Amodt. You like to read?"

"Yeah," I say, though I don't much.

He waves around at the metal shelves. "I've got tons of books, magazines, comics, manga, and graphic novels, but I've got a major problem. These shelves are too full, and my job is to get these out of here and into students' hands. I expect you to check out your share next year."

"I will."

"What do you like to do, Jackson?" Mr. Amodt takes off his glasses and sets them on the desk.

"I love baseball."

"Me, too. We have some excellent baseball books over there." He points to a section. "Have you read *The Boy Who Saved Baseball*?"

"No." I shake my head.

"That's very good. I think you'd like it." He rolls over a stack of ancient books on a cart. "We also do a project where students take apart an old book. You get to cut it up."

"Really? We get to destroy a book?"

"Yeah, one that's no longer in circulation. They'd just be thrown out. So instead you take an X-Acto knife to the spine to see how they are put together."

"Cool."

Gig bursts through the door. "What happened to you?"

"I got lost."

"Let's go. The group is waiting for you and Norquist is steaming mad."

"Thanks." I wave to Mr. Amodt, and Gig and I hurry out the door. "Gig, listen, I saw something." My hands are shaking so I jam them in my pockets.

"What?"

"I saw that ghost of the dead sixth grader."

"Yeah, right."

"I really did. She's gorgeous and she wanted me to follow her."

He turns to me. "Maybe you should have. A ghost might be as close as you'll get to having a girlfriend."

*T*hat evening at game time, my stomach still feels like it could spew, but I've got to play. I can't let my teammates down the first game of the season. I unwrap a piece of bubble gum. Maybe chewing it will help.

"Here's the batting order to start us off." Coach reads from a card that he's clipped to the fence: "Gig bats leadoff. Jackson, you're second. Isaac, third, and Diego is cleanup. Let's get some runs on the board."

I grab my aluminum bat from the rack, slide the weight on, and swing it in the on-deck circle.

"Let's go, Jackson." G-Man's in the bleachers behind our dugout. I haven't talked to him since I decided not to try out for the traveling team. He's sitting by Isaac's mom, examining a sweater she's knitting.

Gig adjusts his red helmet, tightens his batting glove, and digs in. On the first pitch of the season, he swings and laces a single up the middle.

"Good rip, Gig." I take the weight off my bat. At the end of the bench, Sydney claps for him. I take a couple of practice swings and step into the batter's box. Up until now, it's just been practice. I'm ready for the real deal.

The pitcher for the Cheetahs winds up and throws a

fastball down the inside half of the plate. I swing as hard as I can and smash it into the outfield gap. I put my head down and sprint to first. The centerfielder races over to cut off the ball and fires to home. Gig holds at third, while I coast into second with a stand-up double.

"Sweet." Gig claps his hands.

"Way to turn on the pitch," G-Man hollers.

"Bring us in, Isaac." I take off my batting glove and stick it in my back pocket.

But the pitcher doesn't give Isaac anything to hit. He misses outside three times and then throws a ball down in the dirt. The catcher slides over to smother it to prevent a passed ball, as Gig dances down the baseline from third. Isaac tosses his bat aside and jogs to first.

Bases loaded for Diego. "Ducks on the pond." I've always liked that expression for runners on base.

"Meat on the table." Gig claps.

Diego digs in on the left side against the right-handed pitcher. He might even be better from this side than the other.

The pitcher winds up and throws.

"Ball one," the umpire says.

"We want a pitcher, not a belly itcher." Gig jumps off the base and scratches his belly.

The pitcher steps off the mound and wipes his forehead. He has to throw a strike. He can't walk Diego with the bases full.

"Wait for your pitch, Diego." G-Man claps.

Diego takes a smooth practice swing.

The pitcher steps back in, winds, and throws. Diego cracks the ball hard down the right-field line, and I take off running. I round third and race home.

I bump fists with Gig at the plate and we turn to see Isaac heading home. We both wave our hands for him to slide. His foot brushes the plate in a spray of sand just ahead of the throw.

Diego jogs to second with a big smile on his face. A three-run double—what a way to start the season.

"Way to go, Diego," I holler.

He gives me a thumbs-up. Our secret weapon delivers.

CHAPTER 14

"Let's go, Big Gig." We're warming up in the field in the bottom of the first inning. Six to nothing—excellent way to start the game.

"Jackson." Diego throws me a grounder and I bend down to grab it. I smoke the throw back to him at first.

"Second," Hauser calls out.

I run over to cover and Hauser delivers the ball on the corner of the bag. I swipe the tag on an imaginary runner and flip to Sydney, who's backing me up. She throws to Cerrato, as Gig digs in at the mound.

"Batter up," the umpire calls.

"One-two-three inning." I smooth the dirt in front of me as the first batter steps into the box. I smell my freshly cleaned uniform, bubble gum, and grass—the smells of baseball. Gig whips the first pitch in for a strike.

"That a way, Gig," I holler. He might miss school, but he'd never miss a game.

He winds up and throws another bullet. The batter swings late for strike two.

"Give him the heat," Isaac shouts.

The batter waves lamely at the next pitch.

"Strike three," the umpire shouts.

"Way to fire, Rocket Man." I hold up my index finger to indicate one out.

On the next pitch, the batter hits a high pop fly.

"I got it," I shout as I move back onto the outfield grass. The ball keeps floating higher and I keep moving back. "I got it," I yell louder.

As the ball falls, I realize it's deeper than I thought. I hurry back, but the ball bounces off my outstretched glove. I turn to chase it, but Isaac picks it up and fires it in to hold the runner.

How embarrassing. Everybody was watching me, and I didn't make the catch.

"Isaac, that's your ball," Coach Wilkins says. "The center fielder has to call the infielder off."

I tap my chest to let him know it's my mistake. I shouldn't have said I had it. It's nice of Coach not to call me out. He's fair that way. He treats Isaac like a regular team member, not like someone who deserves special treatment just because he's the coach's son.

I move a step closer to second. We could use a double play to bail me out.

Gig winds up and fires a strike. "Way to burn." I pound my glove.

He throws again and the batter hits a two-hopper to the hole. I move right, backhand it, and throw to second. Sydney grabs it and tries to throw to first, but the runner barrels into her and knocks her over. She falls to the ground but hangs on to the ball.

"You okay?" I run over to help her, but she's already jogging back to her spot.

"Nice pink glove," someone on the other team hollers.

"Where can I get one like that?"

Sydney ignores them and gets down in her stance.

Gig shakes his head and stomps around the mound like an angry elephant.

"Two out," Coach calls.

Gig rears back and throws.

"Strike one," the umpire calls.

Gig blazes another strike.

"Strike two."

It looks like he's taking his frustration out on the batter.

"Strike three."

"That's the way, Gig." I run in and pat him on the back. "They can't hit you."

He glares at me and doesn't respond.

With two outs, Hauser throws his catcher's mask to the side and chases a foul pop-up for the final out of the game. He moves left, right, and then left again as the ball comes down. As he reaches for it, he steps on his mask and topples over. The ball drops behind him, and he grabs his ankle.

"Are you okay?" Coach rushes onto the field.

"My ankle," he moans. "I think it's broken."

"It's probably just a sprain." Coach touches it lightly. "Jackson, Gig, come help Hauser to the bench."

Gig and I pull him up. Hauser hangs on to our shoulders and hops over to the bench.

"Trenton, we need a catcher. Can you play catcher for one out?"

"Sure. I've never caught before, but I can do it."

Hauser peels off the catching gear and Trenton puts it on. Meanwhile, Gig, who's now playing first, throws grounders to keep us loose. I look out at the scoreboard. Eleven to three. Gig and Diego have pitched great and I've gotten three hits.

Gig throws a fast grounder to Sydney that takes a wild bounce over her glove. She chases it down in the outfield while Gig smirks. Sydney doesn't have any hits, but she hasn't made any errors, either.

Finally Trenton is ready and Diego throws the first pitch right down the middle. It bounces off Trenton's glove.

"Strike one," the umpire calls.

Diego throws the next pitch in the dirt and the batter swings. The ball slips past Trenton and rolls to the backstop. It doesn't look like he can play catcher, either.

"One more," I holler. "Take him yourself."

Diego winds up and throws a fastball down and away. The batter swings and misses.

"Strike three," the umpire calls.

"Yeah." I race to the mound to congratulate Diego. Gig lifts him off the ground and Isaac races in from the outfield. Over by the fence, G-Man has his hand on Sydney's shoulder and is talking to her. What's he up to?

After we shake hands with the Cheetahs, I go up to G-Man.

"Good game, Jackson. You knocked the ball around the park."

"Thanks."

"That double play with your new second baseman needs some work, though. Ten o'clock tomorrow at the practice field. Does that work?"

"With her?"

"She's your second baseman now. You and Sportelli had to practice to get the timing down."

"I don't know." I turn around to make sure Gig's not listening.

"Be there," G-Man says.

When I walk into the White Horse in my dirty uniform, the hostess gives me a rude look. Why do I have to meet them here? I'd rather go home and eat pizza in front of the TV. After a game, I want to relax, not to be forced to be friendly to people I don't know.

"Over here." Mom stands and waves. She's gotten her hair cut and has bright red polish on her long nails.

Sitting at a round table are Quinn, Mom, a guy, and two girls in fancy dresses.

"I'm Ted." The man wearing a jacket, an orange tie, and a toothy smile stands up. "You must be Jackson. I've heard so much about you." He's talking too fast already. "Great to meet you." He holds out his hand.

I shake, and he puts his other hand on top like he's locking me in a trap.

Mom gives me a big hug that I squeeze out of. I've told her a million times not to do that in public. "How was the game?"

"We won by eight." I sit down next to Quinn.

"And how was your middle school visit?"

"Fine."

"Let me introduce you to Heather and Haley." Mom gestures at them. "Girls, this is Jackson."

I mumble hello and pick up the menu. My stomach has finally settled down and I'm starving.

"We were all discussing our favorite ice creams," Mom says enthusiastically. "What's yours?"

"I don't know."

"Oh, come on, Jackson. Pick one." I hear the edge in her voice.

"Rocky Road." I say the first flavor that pops into my mind.

"That's a good one." Ted grins like a jack-o'-lantern. "I love Rocky Road."

The waitress comes over and I order a cheeseburger and fries, while Ted switches the conversation to favorite candy bars. How am I going to practice tomorrow without Gig knowing? He'll kill me if he finds out.

Ted's yapping excitedly about whether to choose Twix or Whachamacallit, so I turn to Quinn.

"I saw a ghost today."

His eyes widen. "Really?"

"At Longview." I nod. "A real ghost and she wanted me to come with her."

"What for?"

"I don't know."

"What's your favorite, Jackson?" Ted asks.

"Snickers."

"Amazing. That's mine, too." He leans forward. "I never played much baseball. I'm more into golf. But I'm sure I could throw the ball around a bit if you'd like."

"No, thanks." I squeeze my hands under the table and avoid Mom's glare. "I practice with my grandpa."

Ted sticks out his lower lip and glances at Mom. I don't care. I am practicing with G-Man tomorrow.

CHAPTER 15

Saturday is one of those warm, no-clouds-in-the-sky days that are great for baseball. Today, though, I'd prefer thunder and lightning. A tornado would be even better.

Sydney's listening to G-Man's stories about playing ball in the olden days when I get to the field. I thought he might be put off by a girl with a pink glove, but the two of them are laughing like they've been best friends for years.

"Hi, Jackson." Sydney smiles.

"Hey." I hope she was smart enough to keep this secret from Gig.

"Let's get to work before it gets too hot," G-Man says.

We walk out to second base and G-Man asks for Sydney's glove. "Sydney, you're standing in place on the double play." He puts the glove on his hand like there's nothing weird about him wearing a pink glove. "You're a sitting duck for the base runner. They're going to clobber you. You need to move across the bag. "Like this." He steps on the base with his right foot, moves across, and pretends to throw to first.

Sydney watches intently.

"Practice in slow motion without the ball. It's like a dance." He demonstrates again. "One, two, three."

G-Man hands the glove back to Sydney and she practices moving across the base. She's a little awkward at first but gets better.

"Jackson, it's different when you come from shortstop. You want to reach to catch the ball as you're putting your right foot on the bag and then fire to first." G-Man demonstrates the move. "Try that."

I take my position at short and move through the steps in slow motion.

"That's it," G-Man says. "It's important that you throw the ball so that it arrives exactly as your partner is crossing second base.

Sydney and I both nod.

"And put it right at chest level where the glove is."

I glance over at Sydney's chest, which is a lot different from Sportelli's.

"Don't make your partner move the glove because it disrupts the rhythm," G-Man says. "It ruins the dance."

G-Man practiced these double plays with Sportelli and me last year, but I don't remember him going on about it being a dance then.

"Practice flipping the ball to each other as you cross the base," he says. "Short flips. Work on the timing."

I take a couple of steps toward the base, and G-Man hands me a baseball. "Medium speed," he says.

Sydney moves toward the base and I flip the ball. She catches it and then takes it out of her glove to throw.

"Sydney, keep your right hand up by your glove as you cross the base," G-Man says. "That way, you're ready to throw. It's only a fraction of a second difference, but sometimes that's all you need to get the runner out at first."

We practice it over and over. Sydney gets the footwork down and then practices her flips to me. Part of it is just getting used to how the other person moves, how she approaches the base, and where she likes the ball.

"Now let's try it with batted balls," G-Man says. He walks to the bench to pick up the bat, and I slide over to Sydney.

"You didn't tell Gig what you were doing today, did you?"

"Of course not." She shakes her head and her ponytail, which is sticking out of her cap, bounces back and forth.

"I'll start by hitting some close to the bag." G-Man hits grounder after grounder. Sydney catches everything and her throws are accurate. She's not Sportelli, but she's pretty good.

"Now, let's try that play in the hole." G-Man points. "Jackson, throw to the base. Sydney, catch it as you're going across and then plant your foot."

We practice it over and over. Sydney doesn't complain about the repetition or any of G-Man's corrections to her.

"Now we'll try it on a ball toward first," he says. "Sydney, you've got to catch it, spin, and throw to second."

She's listening closely, following everything he says. That's exactly what he wants in a practice player.

G-Man hits balls and she hustles after every one. He hits them farther and farther from her. On the last one, she dives, hops up, and makes a strong throw.

"I like it," he says. "Good work. Come in for water."

As we jog in, a shape on the hill ducks behind a tree. I keep my eye on the spot, but don't see any more movement. A ghost yesterday and a shape today. Am I starting to hallucinate? Am I losing my mind?

Afterward, G-Man works with Sydney on her hitting. "When you're batting ninth, you can be an extra leadoff hitter. Your job is to get on base any way you can so the top of the order can drive you in."

She takes a big practice swing.

"Shorten that swing up, Sydney," G-Man says. "Nice compact stroke. Crouch down. Make it difficult for the pitcher to throw strikes to you. And move up on the plate. You'd be willing to get hit by a pitch now and then in order to get a free base, wouldn't you?"

"Yes."

"I thought so. Make yourself a tough out and increase your on-base percentage. With those four hitters after you, if you get on base, you'll score some runs."

"Thanks, G-Man," Sydney says.

"No problem." G-Man walks out to the mound.

She turns to me. "I've never had anyone coach me like this. That's another reason I wanted to play baseball. To get better."

I walk out to short. She works hard and is determined to improve, but if Gig saw me here with her, he'd kill me.

Chapter

"**H**appy Mother's Day," Quinn and I shout together as we burst into Mom's room, carrying cards and presents.

"What do you two have?" Mom sits up in bed in her light blue nightgown and brushes her hair back with her hand. Light streams through the wide windows that look over the lake.

"I made a card for you." I hand her the folded green construction paper with a metallic marker drawing of an eye, a heart, and the letter U.

She opens it up and reads out loud:

Dear Mom,
HAPPY MOTHER'S DAY. Thank you for everything you've done for me. Thank you for being an awesome mom.

I am sorry for the times I've messed up. I hope you have the best mother's day ever.
Love,
Jackson

She looks up at me. "Thank you, Jackson. I am so lucky to be your mother."

"Here's mine." Quinn holds out the card he made at school.

Mom examines the cut-paper picture of tiny stars on the front. "Beautiful." She opens it. "'To the best mother in the universe. Love, Quinn.'" She wipes the corner of her eye. "Thank you, Quinny."

"Open my present first." He hands her his package wrapped in sparkly purple paper.

Mom slices through the tape with her red fingernails. "It's heavy. What is it?"

"A paperweight," he shouts. "I made it."

Mom examines a white glazed square of clay with two hearts on top and his name carved into the bottom. "Oh, Quinn, I love it. Come here and give me a hug."

Quinn moves closer and Mom wraps him up and kisses him on the cheek.

"For you." I hand Mom the box wrapped in butterfly paper.

"That's wonderfully wrapped." She runs her hand along the smooth paper. "Did you do it yourself?"

"Yep, first thing this morning."

"What is it?" She examines the rectangular package. "Too small for a tablecloth, too big for a pair of earrings." She shakes it. "Not a new car."

"Mom." Quinn laughs.

"It sure smells good." She unwraps it slowly. "How beautiful. You know how much I love candles." She holds it up to her nose. "Mocha cinnamon. I love it. Come here, Jackson."

I walk next to Quinn beside the bed and she gives me a hug and a kiss on the cheek. "You boys are so wonderful." She wipes her eyes that have gone watery. "You are the two best things that ever happened to me."

At the pool on Sunday, I sit in the hot tub with Dad, while Quinn dangles his feet over the side. Dad rubs his eyes. He looks tired like he usually does after working late on Saturday night.

"How come G-Man isn't here?" Quinn leans over and moves his plastic fish through the water.

"He had a collectors' meeting this afternoon."

I lean back against the hot tub jet. After getting up early, I'm tired, too.

"Dad." I stretch my feet out. "Did you play a lot of baseball as a kid?"

"Sure," he says, "but I always liked soccer better."

"Why?"

"I loved the movement of it. Baseball was more standing around. And because your grandpa had been such a big baseball star, he was very demanding. There's no way I could live up to his expectations, so I found my own game. He didn't know anything about soccer. He still doesn't. I'm sure that's one reason I chose it."

"Was G-Man more demanding than he is now?"

"Are you kidding?" Dad sits forward. "You have no idea how much he's mellowed."

"What's mellow?" Quinn looks up from his fish.

"Relaxed," Dad says. "I'm sure that's why I chose cooking, too. My dad didn't know anything about that, either. I got that from my mom. You don't remember her very well, do you?"

"Just a little." I have vague memories of Grandma pretending to vacuum my feet and playing Legos with me. She let me pretend the Legos were food, and we put them in the oven. She died from cancer when I was four, younger than Quinn is now. That's pretty small.

"She would have loved spending time with you," Dad says. "I'm sorry she didn't get a chance to see you boys grow up."

"But G-Man does." Quinn splashes water with his feet.

"Yup." Dad climbs out. "Let's go slide."

*H*auser hops around on crutches at practice on Monday. "I told you it was broken, and none of you believed me," he says. "Do you want to sign my cast?"

"Sure." I take his blue Sharpie and write my name and my number 12. "How long are you out?"

"Two months, the whole season." Hauser seems kind of proud, as Sydney and Isaac squeeze in to sign the cast. Like getting injured is some kind of big accomplishment.

"Jackson." Coach Wilkins calls me over. "We need a catcher with Hauser out. You've got good hands. You understand the game. And you work well with Gig and Diego. I'd like you to try catcher today."

"But what about short?" I can't believe it. I finally get to play short—my favorite position—and he wants me to give it up.

"I'll move Isaac in."

"But I've never caught before."

"Give it a try." He leads me to the bench. "Here's the stuff."

I sit down and snap a shin guard on. I don't want to catch. I feel like I'm a knight putting on armor for a battle I don't want to fight.

"You'll do fine." Coach hands me the chest protector and I swing it over my head and snap it behind my back. "You've got to have one of these." Coach takes a hard plastic triangle out of his bag. "Use this cup to protect your family jewels."

I turn away so Sydney won't see me shoving it in my pants. Why can't somebody else catch? Why do I have to do it?

I put the helmet on, pull the mask down, and pick up the catcher's mitt. It feels huge, like I'm wearing a garbage can lid. I already miss my regular glove. I flex the mitt a couple of times as I stagger to home plate. Why does Isaac get to play short? He's got good hands, too. He could be the catcher.

"You look good." Diego steps to the plate as first batter.

"Yeah, right." I crouch down. Gig winds up and fires a fastball outside that pops my glove. I throw the ball back to him. It's weird to sit back here and see everybody in front of me. Isaac at short points to Sydney at second. That's the weirdest—to see somebody else playing short. That's my position.

Gig blazes an inside pitch and Diego steps back. I reach to catch it. Maybe I should drop some of these, let some of them get by me the way Trenton did. Maybe if I do a bad job, I can move back to short.

Gig bounces the next pitch in the dirt, and I instinctively fall to my knees and smother the ball.

"Good block." Coach claps.

I throw the ball back to Gig. What's the matter with him? He hasn't thrown a strike yet.

"Hit the mitt, Gig," Coach says. "Fire it in there."

I bend into my crouch and Gig winds up. The next pitch is so wild, I leap up and stretch my glove but still can't grab it. The ball clangs against the fence.

"Jackson," Coach says. "Go talk with your pitcher. Settle him down."

I take off my mask and walk out to the mound. Gig turns his back to me and rubs the baseball.

"Hey, what's the matter?" I stand next to him.

"Like you don't know."

"What?"

"Don't play stupid with me."

"What are you talking about?"

"You practiced with Squid Face on Saturday, didn't you?"

"Nnn . . . ," I start to lie, but I can tell from the tight look on his face that he knows. How did he find out? "Yeah." I look down.

"How could you?"

"G-Man set it up. I couldn't get out of it." I look over at Sydney, who's talking with Isaac. "Gig, she's on our team. She's not quitting. You need to deal with it."

"You double-crossed me."

"She's playing second. We needed to work on the double play."

"Hey, guys," Coach hollers. "What's going on?"

"Nothing," Gig spits out.

I trudge back to the plate. More like everything.

CHAPTER 17

I'm running through the woods with Diego, Isaac, and Gig, and I'm holding a shiny new baseball in my glove. We're late so we take the shortcut to our game at Echo Park. Gig's in the lead, followed by Isaac and Diego, then me. We're all pumped up about the upcoming game against the Jaguars.

Suddenly clouds darken and rain falls. I struggle to keep up, but it's hard to see, and I get separated from them. Up ahead I hear voices arguing about where to take cover, but I can't catch up no matter how hard I run. My legs feel like they're moving in slow motion. The rain pounds faster and I'm afraid our game will be canceled.

At the bottom of the hill, I step in some mud and my left foot is stuck. My whole shoe disappears, and when I try to pull it out, my leg gets sucked in deeper. My other foot gets sucked in, too. It feels like quicksand. Both shoes fill with water and I'm pulled deeper. The more I struggle, the worse it gets and soon everything below my knees has disappeared into the earth. I have the weird sensation that roots are running out from my feet and I'm turning into a tree.

Thunder rumbles and rain whips down. Where are the guys? How come they didn't come back for me? I'm shivering as the sky gets blacker. There's no way we'll get the game in. I feel the squishiness of the mud, and now I'm sucked in up to my waist. I listen closely but can't hear anyone.

Lightning cracks and lights up the unfamiliar ground. I check my glove—empty. I look around. The new baseball is sinking into the mud. I must have dropped it. E-6. Error on the shortstop.

Another flash of lightning and I feel an intense pain. A blast of heat rips through me, and I smell burning. I've been split in two.

I struggle awake and burrow my head in my pillow. It's only a dream, but it's creepy. The dream felt more real than I feel now. I wrap myself in my comforter and toss and turn.

I'm drained, like I didn't sleep at all. I check the clock. Time to get up, but I can't. I don't want to get dressed. I don't want to go to school. I don't want to think about any more things splitting up.

As we line up for art, kids carry all kinds of junk. I completely forgot the homework. I rush over to the trash can and grab an orange peel, a licorice wrapper, and two empty Mini Pringles cans.

"Line up, Jackson," Mrs. Spanier says. "You need to plan your work and work your plan, not wait until the last minute. If you fail to plan, you plan to fail."

Yeah, right. I go to the end of the line behind Gig. He hasn't talked to me all day. I hate this stupid silent treatment. He should realize that if Sydney quit, Trenton would have to play second. None of us wants that.

Ms. Langley has added even more junk to her pile in the art room. "Take anything that looks interesting to you." Today she's wearing glasses with silver frames that sparkle.

I grab a toilet paper roll and hold it up to Gig. Normally he'd make a joke, but he's ignoring me. He's busy folding a piece of bubble wrap around three large keys. He takes his stuff to a seat on the other side of the room from where we usually sit. The big baby.

"Alter your objects any way you'd like," Ms. Langley says. "Bend them, squish them, twist them, cut them. Experiment with them and lay them out to see how they look before you use the glue guns."

I grab scissors and start cutting up the Pringles cans. The bottoms look like they could be eyes. I pull back the cardboard and trim them neatly. I set the toilet paper roll down as a mouth, but it doesn't look right. I crumple it and turn it. It works better as a nose. I tear the red licorice wrapper. That works as a mouth.

I walk back to the pile and sort through the strange stuff. I pick out two speckled seashells and a handful of twigs.

At my table, I turn over the seashells and place them as ears. The twigs will work for hair. All I have left is the orange peel. I could throw that away. Or I could find a spot for it. How about some eyebrows? I start gluing objects and get lost in the project. I gaze into the potato-chip-can eyes, and they stare back.

It's strange, but for a second, I really do feel like I'm looking at myself.

"Jackson, you did a good job yesterday." Coach Wilkins hands me the gear. "We really need you at catcher."

He didn't even ask me about it. I look out at second base where Sydney is demonstrating to Isaac how to hold up both hands on the double play ball. That's not fair. That's what G-Man showed her when we were practicing together.

I snap on the bulky shin guards and the straps form two Xs on the back of my legs. Maybe Coach wanted Isaac to play short all along. Maybe having me catch was a way to open up the position for him. Maybe he *is* favoring his son.

I throw the chest protector over my head and snap it behind my back. I didn't bring my cup. I thought someone else would catch. Since I don't want to ask Coach for another one, I'll be careful and play without one.

"Let's have some batting practice." Coach puts on his glove and walks to the mound. "Gig, you bat first."

Gig grabs the red bat, takes a couple of swings, and steps to the plate.

"What's up?" I bend down in my crouch.

Gig digs in at the box and doesn't say anything.

"Stupid baby," I mutter under my breath.

Gig concentrates on Coach, whose first pitch is in the dirt. I slide over to block it.

"Good stop, Jackson," he says.

On the next pitch, Gig takes a big cut and whacks my glove.

"Owww." I take off the glove and shake out my hand. "What are you doing?"

"You're too close," he says. "Move back."

"You're too far back in the box."

"No, I'm not."

"Gig, move up a bit," Coach calls.

"Big wimp." Gig digs in again.

"Shut up." I squat down.

Gig swings on the next pitch and the foul tip smacks my mask. I take it off and shake my head. There's no way he tried to do that, but it feels like he did. I put the mask back on and slowly squat back into position.

Gig smashes the next pitch to short and Isaac bobbles the ball. That's where I should be, not back here getting all beat up.

Coach winds up and throws and Gig ticks a foul that bounces off the ground and hits me on the inside of the thigh before I can get my glove down. That was way too close. I need to remember that cup for next time. I squeeze my legs together and the spot stings. I hate catching.

———

"Infield practice." Coach walks to the plate holding three balls and a bat. "Jackson, go down to the bullpen and warm up Gig. Take it easy. We've got a game tomorrow."

I watch Sydney charge a slow roller and pick it up barehanded and flip to Diego.

"Get a move on, Jackson," Coach calls.

He knows I'd rather be at shortstop fielding ground balls than being sent out to the bullpen with Gig. Who ever imagined our friendship would be wrecked by a girl? A girl that's his sister!

I put on my mask and bend down. Gig blazes the first pitch and my glove pops. He fires another. Coach said to take it easy. I should go out and tell him to relax, to lighten up, to save himself for the game tomorrow.

But that's hard to do when we're not talking.

CHAPTER 18

"'**A** fantabulous night to make romance,'" G-Man sings along to the radio as he takes Quinn and me out for ice cream.

"What's 'fantabulous' mean?" Quinn asks.

"It's a combination of 'fantastic' and 'fabulous.'" G-Man turns the volume up and taps the steering wheel to the beat. "It means 'really good.'"

"Fantabulous," Quinn says.

"Your grandma loved this song." G-Man smiles. "And since she loved it, I love it." G-Man sings along loudly to the rest of the song.

"You going with the kiddie cone of chocolate, Quinnster?" G-Man looks in the rearview mirror.

"Yes, it's fantabulous."

"What about you, Jackson?"

"One scoop of Black Hills Gold and one of Heath Bar Crumble."

"That's a good combo." G-Man pulls into a spot right in front of Sunny's. "I'm going for Mud Pie and Almond Delight."

The line is long on a hot evening that feels like the middle of summer. I wish we were done with school, and I didn't have to study for a stupid spelling test tonight.

I sit between Quinn and G-Man on the brick wall outside as we eat our cones. "Coach Wilkins made me catcher with Hauser out."

"Excellent," G-Man says.

"No, it's not. I'd rather be at short."

"Catcher's the best position," G-Man says. "That's what I played. You're involved with every pitch. You see what's happening all over the field. And you work with your pitcher to help him throw the best game possible."

I chew a chunk of Heath Bar.

"And you can talk to the other team's batters," G-Man says. "You can say things that throw them off their game."

"Like what?"

"Flattery works. Tell them what great hitters they are.

Some guys start thinking they're stars and forget to concentrate on the pitch. The next thing you know they're back on the bench after striking out."

"I don't know if they allow that."

"How are they going to prohibit saying someone is a great hitter?" G-Man asks. "By the way, how's Sydney doing?"

"Fine." I take a bite of waffle cone. I don't want to talk about her.

"She can play," G-Man says. "Years ago, girls never got a chance like that. Your grandma was a good athlete and she liked baseball, but she never got the opportunity to be on a team."

I wipe my chin with my paper napkin.

"I read an interesting article in the paper this morning," G-Man says. "There's been a big increase in serious injuries among young athletes. Guess what they said was one of the major causes?"

"What?" I look up.

"Specializing in one sport at a young age. Doctors say the emphasis on specialization and traveling teams is putting too much strain on kids."

"Traveling teams?" I smile.

"Yeah, they said the best thing for growing bodies is to

play different sports during the year to use different muscles. That's what we all did when I was your age."

"That's what I do now."

"That's wise. You're a smart kid, Jackson."

"What about me?" Quinn says.

"You're smart, too." G-Man rubs Quinn's head. "Two smart kids."

"I found it." Quinn scoops out the malted milk ball from the bottom of his cone.

"Toss it in the lot," G-Man says.

Quinn swings his arm forward, but the malted milk ball lands a couple of feet from the curb.

"I'll help it." I walk over and kick it into the parking lot.

"That's too far," Quinn says.

"No, it's not. Just wait."

We watch cars pull out and drive past as we finish our cones. "Yay!" we all cheer when an SUV runs over it and the malted milk ball pops.

"**A**s you've noticed, all our spelling words in this week's quiz are careers," Mrs. Spanier says. "It's never too early to start thinking about your future."

Physician.

Meteorologist. Is that two Os or three?

Gastroenterologist. Is it an E or an I? I studied these, but I still can't remember. I hate spelling.

"Pass your papers in. I hope you all did well," Mrs. Spanier says. "Speaking of careers, tomorrow Mr. Selby, the writer I mentioned, is coming to our class. I'm sure he will stress how important spelling is if you want to be a good writer. Remember, I expect high-standard behavior when we have a guest in our classroom."

Snuffy goes on and on with her high-standard speech and how it's the secret to a successful career, like being a meteorologist. I look out the window at the sun shining. Any meteorologist in America could tell you that I'd rather be outside playing ball.

*T*he guys on the Jaguars start in on their talk in the first inning.

"It's so cutsey cute."

"Why don't all of you wear pink gloves?"

"Girly guys on a loser team."

"Shut up." Gig spits on the mound.

"Just ignore it," Coach Wilkins says. "Let's play ball."

Everybody tries, but it's hard when they keep talking. Just

because these guys have been league champs three years in a row, they think they're better than anyone else.

Gig's throwing hard, but he's missing my target and giving up walks.

In the second inning when Sydney comes to bat, the chatter increases.

"How come you don't use a pink bat?"

"What about a pink helmet?"

"And a pink dress. You should play in a dress."

Sydney crouches down and pretends to tune it out, but it's got to be difficult to have a group of loudmouths watching your every move and making smart remarks.

She strikes out on three pitches to end the inning.

"Go paint your nails."

"Boys rule. Girls drool."

*I*n the last inning, Diego's throwing heat as he tries to keep the score close. He gives up a walk to the first batter and then concentrates on the second. He throws a pitch inside that the batter hits to short. Isaac stabs the high hop and throws to Sydney at second. She crosses the base and sets to throw.

The runner veers out of the baseline and slides into her.

"Hey, what are you doing?" Isaac runs over.

"Just a hard slide." The runner hops up.

"You're way out of line." Isaac offers a hand and pulls Sydney up.

She brushes herself off and limps back to her position.

I go out to the mound. "One more out, Diego. Strike out this jerk. We'll come back and get some runs to win it."

He nods.

The big guy, who's been the mouthiest, digs in at the plate.

"Great hitter." I try G-Man's technique. "He can hit to all fields."

The batter turns to me and smirks.

Whoosh. Diego whistles a fastball at his head and the guy falls to the ground.

"Ball one," the umpire says.

"He wasn't aiming for your head," I tell the batter. "He can't control it."

The batter steps back in cautiously. Diego delivers the next pitch down the middle and the batter doesn't swing.

"Strike one."

"Really good hitter," I call.

He watches another one go by.

"Strike two."

I point my finger outside as a signal to Diego. Let's see if this guy will chase one.

Diego nods and I slide over. He fires at my glove. The batter tries to hold up, but can't stop his swing.

"Strike three," the umpire hollers.

"That's the way to bring it." I point to Diego. "Let's get some hits." I peel off my chest protector. "I'm up first."

Our last at bat. Down by three. We need a big rally.

CHAPTER

"**B**atter up." The umpire bends down and brushes sand off home plate.

"Make him pitch to you," G-Man calls. He's sitting between Quinn and Dad in the bleachers.

I step in and remind myself to be patient even though I'm ready to swing. I let the first pitch go for a ball.

The second one is low, too.

I'm ready for a strike now, as I take a practice swing. The pitcher winds up and throws down the middle. I swing and hit a looper to left. I race to first as it drops in for a hit.

"That's the way to get it started." Coach Wilkins claps.

Isaac laces a single to center on the first pitch and I hold at second. There's no sense taking a chance of getting thrown out at third when we need base runners for Diego.

He strides to the plate and steps into the left-handed batter's box.

"Bring us in," I call.

Diego takes three pitches for balls. He doesn't chase bad pitches and forces the pitcher to throw something good to him.

The next pitch is grooved down the middle and Diego attacks it. The ball smacks off the fence in right as I race around third base. Isaac flies in after me and we bump fists. Diego slides into third with a triple.

"Awesome." Hauser, who's standing on his crutches, claps.

Down by one with the tying run at third and no outs. We can do this. We can rally to win. We can finally get revenge on the Jaguars.

Strikeouts to Cerrato and Trenton sandwiched around walks to Gunderson and Stein, however, leave Diego stranded at third. Bases are loaded, but we're down to our last batter, and it's Sydney.

She walks to the plate, and she's still limping from that earlier collision at second.

Their pitcher grins and throws the first pitch high and inside. Sydney ducks to avoid getting hit in the head and the pitcher laughs.

"C'mon, Sydney," Coach says. "You can do it."

After another ball and two strikes, Sydney is down to her last strike. She digs in and gets ready.

The pitcher throws a fastball and Sydney swings and hits a roller down the first base line that curves foul at the last minute.

"Got a piece of it. That's the way to stay alive." Isaac claps.

I clap, too, but don't say anything because Gig's right in front of me in the on-deck circle. If Sydney gets on, he can drive home the winning run.

She takes a short practice swing.

The pitcher throws down and away and Sydney swings and misses.

"Strike three," the umpire says. "That's the ball game."

Gig smashes his bat down. Diego flips his helmet off and shakes his head. That pitch might have been a ball, but it was too close to take with two strikes.

"Let it go, Syd," Coach calls out as she trudges back to the dugout. "Tough at-bat."

Isaac meets her and takes the bat. "We'll get 'em next time."

Gig kicks a batting helmet like it's a football.

"Get it under control, Gig," Coach says sternly.

I pick up the catching equipment and shove it in the blue bag. It hurts to lose a close one like that. Especially to the Jaguars.

*T*he visiting writer isn't anything like what I expected. He's a tall black man with a shaved head and a goatee, who says we can call him by his first name, Hayes. He shows us samples of his first drafts that are sloppy with crossed-out words and things written on the sides. "The first draft is fast." He rolls up his sleeves. "Forget about being perfect. What we need are some words on the page."

Mrs. Spanier sits at her desk and scrunches her lips together.

"On the first draft, we want a story with interesting characters." Hayes stretches out on the chair in front. "We're not worried about spelling, punctuation, or grammar."

Mrs. Spanier sniffs loudly. Maybe this wasn't what she expected, either.

"I'm going to give you a topic and we're all going to write a story for tomorrow," Hayes says. "Make up your own superhero. What will he or she look like? What will it do? What special qualities will he or she or it have? One request: Create your own character. Don't take one from TV or the movies." Hayes stands and walks around the room. "Let's try this. Everybody close your eyes. Relax and watch what names of characters come into your mind."

When I close my eyes I'm surprised that I start seeing names of characters: Eraser Man, Mister Freeze, Captain Baseball.

"Your mind is full of ideas," Hayes says. "Let them flow. Think of your own life, of things you'd like to do better. What special powers would you like to have?"

Bigger. I'd like to be bigger and stronger.

"Open your eyes," Hayes says. "On your paper, I want you to write down the first idea that pops into your head."

I pick up my pen and write **HOMERUNZILLA**. I don't know what it means or where it came from.

"Don't worry about whether it's good enough." Hayes clasps his hands behind his head. "Don't worry what anyone else will say. Just start writing down some qualities of your character."

Underneath **HOMERUNZILLA**, I start a list.

Ten-year-old boy.
Turns into a monster when it's his turn to bat.

The monster is lime green, fifteen feet tall, and
four hundred pounds.

He has a long spiked tail that he uses to hold
the bat.

HOMERUNZILLA can hit the ball over one
thousand feet.

Likes to chew bubble gum and blow monster
bubbles.

"Without saying anything to anyone," Hayes says, "I want you to start writing about this character. Don't worry. It's only practice. See how fast you can put words on the page." He holds up his index finger. "One, two, three, go."

I start writing about HOMERUNZILLA and his team-mates, TORNADO MAN, THE VACUUM, and SWITCH-ERINO. TORNADO MAN delivers pitches with the power of a storm. THE VACUUM picks up anything hit near him, sucks it in, and ejects a laserlike throw. SWITCHERINO can bat from either side, throw with either hand, and can play any position.

"Once you have characters," Hayes says, "create a problem. Make it something big, something complicated, that can't be solved right away."

I close my eyes to think about a problem. A big game against their main rivals, who are led by a guy who plays all positions at the same time: MULTIPLE MAN.

"How many of you have read the Harry Potter books?" Hayes asks.

I raise my hand along with lots of kids. I've seen the movies.

"When Harry encounters a problem, does he solve it right away?"

"No," we all say.

"What usually happens?"

I raise my hand.

"Yes."

"When he tries to solve it, things usually get worse."

"Exactly." Hayes taps his finger on my desk. "Don't be in a hurry to solve all your problems. Lots of times, things get more complicated."

He doesn't need to remind me. I put my head down and write about HOMERUNZILLA and his problems and how bad things get. I create his coach, CAPTAIN BASEBALL, who tries to help, but makes things worse, too. I write and write and am startled to hear Hayes.

"We have to pause now. Good work. Good start." He rubs his hands together. "For tomorrow, come in with a story with a beginning, middle, and end. Create interesting characters with some big problems. How many of you have computers at home to type these up?"

I raise my hand along with most kids.

"If you can, type these up. Make sure you save and double space," Hayes says. "If you don't have a computer at home, you can go to the library or a friend's house. If you can't, don't worry. Write a new draft by hand and skip every other line. That will help when we revise."

"What if you don't like the character you've got?" Gig asks. "What if he's boring?"

"Change him," Hayes says. "Pick a character that's interesting to you."

I can't remember Gig ever asking a question about writing before.

"He's cool." At recess, we're talking about Hayes, who is working with all the fifth graders.

"Finally a decent topic." Gig pulls at a string on his glove.

"Hayes is fun to have in the classroom," Isaac says.

In six years we've never had a teacher who wasn't white. I've never thought about it until now. Isaac and Diego probably have.

"It's too much work to type it all out." Diego rolls two balls around in his hand.

"You can come over to my house to use our computer," I offer.

"It's not that. We have a computer. I just don't like to type."

"Me neither, but at least it's interesting." I put on my glove. "Snuffy has us type all kinds of boring stuff."

"I still don't know what to write about." Diego juggles the two balls.

"Just pick a problem," I say. "Then create a superhero with powers to solve it."

"I can think of plenty of problems."

"Pick one then. It doesn't have to be perfect."

"Yeah," Gig says. "Or pick something that's part of you and exaggerate it. Like I could choose from SuperBrain or Man That All Girls Dream About Going Out With."

"Dream." Isaac laughs. "More like a nightmare."

After school, Mom picks Quinn and me up.

"Are we going to Target?" Quinn scrambles into the backseat.

"Absolutely." She looks over at me. "I told Quinn he could

pick out a new Matchbox car for doing such good work lately."

"What about me? I've been doing good work, too."

She looks puzzled. "What do you need?"

"A new baseball." I remember my dream of the ball getting sucked into the mud. I haven't been able to find my good ball since then.

At the store, Quinn asks if he can ride in the cart and I'm surprised when Mom says yes and lets me push him.

"We've got to hurry to the toy department." I turn quickly around the corner. "They might run out of cars."

Mom smiles and trails behind us. "Slow down."

While Quinn and Mom examine different cars, I run off to sporting goods to find a baseball. I open the box and smell the fresh leather. I take the ball out and finger the tight stitching. I toss it up and catch it. Just right.

Back at the cart, Quinn shows me his new logging truck.

"I like it."

"You have a game tomorrow, right?" Mom asks.

"Yeah, why?"

"I've been telling Ted and the girls how good you are. They'd like to see you play. Tomorrow would work out well. Is that okay with you?"

"They don't need to come, Mom. G-Man will be there."

"I didn't ask you that." Her mouth tightens. "I asked if it would be okay."

"I don't know."

"Jackson, it's your choice. You can make this harder or easier."

I walk on ahead of them. Every choice I have lately feels harder.

CHAPTER 20

"**G**et her," Gig calls.

At practice, I chase after Sydney in a rundown with Diego. I fake a throw. She freezes and I tag her on the arm.

"Okay, next runner." Coach Wilkins puts his hand on Gig's shoulder.

Gig takes his place halfway between second and first, and Coach throws to Diego, who quickly fires to me. I hold up the ball and chase him back to first like I'm supposed to. When he's almost to the base, I toss the ball to Diego. Gig hits the breaks and turns to run back toward me. Diego throws to me and Gig darts back the other way, like a jackrabbit.

I lunge to tag him and he falls to the ground, rolls over, and dives for the bag.

"Safe," he hollers.

"Make sure you're close enough when you stretch for the tag," Coach says.

Gig jumps up and brushes dirt from his shirt. He's the hardest guy to get out in rundowns.

Sydney stands next to Isaac, concentrating on Coach's base-running instructions. She hasn't acted at all like Gig said she would. She's not trying to tell us how to do things. She's not trying to be in control. She's just playing baseball.

Gig should be able to accept that.

"Let's have you pick a partner to read to," Hayes says. "When you read your story out loud, pay attention to the rhythm. Pay attention to the flow. Cross out any words you don't need and add any you do."

I look over at Gig, who's gesturing at Trenton to be his partner. He's making such an obvious effort to avoid me.

"Raise your hand if you need a partner." Hayes stands up.

I raise my hand and feel like a loser as I look down at my typed paper.

"I'll be your partner, Jackson." Hayes walks over. "You read to me."

I smell Hayes's cologne as he sits down next to me. I read to him about HOMERUNZILLA and his teammates, and Hayes laughs at all the right parts.

"That's a good specific detail about HOMERUNZILLA carrying his tail while he charges around the bases. You create a vivid picture for us."

"Thanks." I like the story. I don't usually feel that way about my writing.

After everybody is finished reading, Hayes writes a word on the board in big letters:

REVISION

"What do you think of when you see this word?" Hayes taps on the whiteboard.

"Checking your work," Gig says.

"Spelling and punctuation," I add.

"What else do you think of with revision?" Hayes looks around the room.

"Being bored to death," Gig says, and everybody, including Hayes, laughs.

"Let's examine the word." Hayes draws a line between

RE and VISION with his marker. "A very simple word with two parts. What's 're' mean, Jackson?"

"To do it again."

"Yes. And what's 'vision' mean?"

"To see. Like night vision."

"Yes. So what does 'revision' mean?"

"To see again," I say hesitantly.

"Exactly." Hayes tosses the marker and catches it. "Revision means to see again, and all of us can do that." He walks around the room. "Everyone, turn the story that you wrote for today over so you can't see it. If you see it, you'll start editing, and that's not what we're doing now. We're doing revision, so take out your writing notebooks."

I pull out my blue notebook and open to a clean page.

"Before we go any further, everybody, set your pen down and quietly stand up." Hayes puts his finger to his lips.

I push my chair back and stand.

"We need to stretch." Hayes extends his arms and almost touches the ceiling. He leads us through a series of stretches for our arms, shoulders, and legs. "When you write, you use your whole body." He grabs his elbows behind his back. "We need to get loosened up."

I look over at Gig, who's smiling. Finally something to do in class that he's really good at.

"Now quietly sit down." Hayes gestures with his hands. "Everybody, close your eyes."

I close my eyes and listen.

"See the main character of your story," Hayes says calmly. "See where it is. See how it is moving. See what size it is. See what it is wearing. See what expression it is making. Now, without saying anything to anyone, open your eyes, and write down everything you just saw."

I write about HOMERUNZILLA sitting in the dugout and covering the whole bench with his big butt. He's wearing his huge yellow baseball shirt and his size thirty-three spikes. He's deep in concentration, as he picks up a streetlight for a bat and tromps to the plate.

"You see how easy it is," Hayes says. "You are seeing your story again. Revision. Let's do it again. Close your eyes and pay attention to what time of day it is. What's the weather like? What does the sky look like?"

I open my eyes and write and write. Hayes asks some more questions and soon I've filled up two whole pages. My story is going to be about twice as long.

"Add these details in and type up a new version of your story for Monday," Hayes says. "Do a good job on this. I talked with Ms. Langley in the art room, and she said she'll help you create covers for your stories when they are finished. You'll make them into books."

He's giving us lots of work, but amazingly we're not complaining the way we usually do.

At recess, Sydney's playing catch with Kelsey and her friends from softball, as Diego, Gig, Isaac, and I run by. She looks up as we take the field. She might like to be out here with us, but that's not possible. The team is one thing; school's something else.

"I'm up first," Gig hollers.

"Do the bat." Isaac tosses it to Gig and he grabs it.

I put my hand on top of his.

Diego puts his next.

Then Isaac.

Gig puts his on top of the knob. "Told you. I bat first."

I'll pitch. I race to the mound and rub my new baseball.

Gig digs in and I throw the first pitch right down the middle. He hammers it into the left-field gap, where Isaac chases after it.

"Good hit," I say.

"Nice pitch." He digs in at the batter's box with his head down.

Four words aren't a lot, but it's a start.

Chapter 21

When I get home, a letter for me is sitting on the kitchen table. I recognize the handwriting on the address: my own. I tear open the envelope and unfold the paper.

Hey FutureMe,

How's the team? What's going on between Gig and Sydney? Are they talking? Ignoring each other?

How are you doing at shortstop? Any errors? Remember, it's the best position on the field and you get to play it this year.

Are you making them throw strikes to you and not chasing bad pitches? Are you making every at-bat count?

You can beat any team in the league. Don't be intimidated by anyone.

Go, Panthers!

Your past self

I reread the letter I sent to myself. I can't believe how much has changed. I don't even play shortstop anymore.

Gig's still not talking most of the time. What's that supposed to accomplish? And what was I supposed to do about Sydney? I thought it might be fun to get a message from my past self, but it's one more reminder of how bad things have gone.

"Leopards are undefeated." Isaac pulls bats out of the black bag and hands them to me.

"I know. Their games haven't even been close." I lean the bats against the fence.

"They think they'll blow us away." Isaac holds the last bat out to me.

"We can beat any team in the league." I take a practice swing. "I got a letter that said that."

"Who from?"

"Myself. I was going to use FutureMe, but it wasn't far enough in the future. You have to send it at least ninety days out, so I used snail mail. It still worked. I sent it to remind me that we can beat them."

"I don't know." Isaac watches the Leopards take infield practice. They look good.

"Hey." Diego and Gig come into the dugout together.

"We can beat these guys," I say.

"Yep." Diego looks confident.

Gig just nods.

I play catch with Isaac as Cerrato, Stein, and our other teammates filter in. The ball smacks my glove and I loosen up my arm on some long throws.

"Let's go, Panthers. Look sharp." G-Man's in the bleachers behind third base. I shake my glove in a wave and he gives me a thumbs-up.

When we take the field for warm-ups, no one is at second.

"Anybody seen Sydney?" Coach asks.

We all shake our heads. Did she quit without telling anyone? Did the pressure finally get to her? I look at Gig. He doesn't seem to know any more than anyone else.

"Trenton, take second." Coach pats him on the back.

Behind the backstop, Mom, Quinn, Ted, and the girls climb the bleachers. The girls are wearing matching yellow dresses and have their hair up like they're going to a party. It's just a baseball game. Why did they have to come?

*T*he first batter hits a pop foul by the opponent's dugout. I toss my mask and race over. "I got it."

"Drop it!" the on-deck batter says.

I circle under it and squeeze the ball tightly. "One out." I hold up my index finger at him and hear G-Man cheering.

Diego misses with two pitches low and steps off the mound to rub the ball. Gig kicks the bag at first. Sydney should have at least told him she was quitting. She should have had the guts to tell all of us.

Gig smacks his glove. He made such a big deal about wanting her to quit, but he doesn't look any happier now.

The next batter laces a line drive into the hole. Isaac dives for it but doesn't come up with it. If I were playing short, I would have had that. He's playing too close to second. I motion to him to move over toward third, and he does.

Diego concentrates and gets two strikes on the next batter. I drop my glove low and inside. Let's see if he can hit that corner.

Diego delivers exactly to the spot.

"Strike three," the umpire calls.

I jump out of my crouch and fire to first, where the runner has drifted too far from the base. Gig grabs the ball and the runner is frozen between bases. Gig fires to Isaac, who chases the runner back to first. He flips to Gig too early, and the runner turns and races to second. Gig throws to Trenton, who swings his glove to apply the tag but drops the ball.

"Safe," the umpire shouts.

Shoot. We had him. We can't afford to give up outs like that.

On the next pitch, the batter hits a bouncer to Trenton. He sticks his glove out and makes the stop, but he throws the ball in the dirt to Gig, who can't scoop it cleanly. Runners at first and third with two out.

"C'mon, Trenton," I shout. We should be out of this inning. He's killing us.

I check their coach at third, who's touching his knees, his hips, and his chest. He's making signs like he's playing some kind of kindergarten game.

The coach whispers something to the base runner. Probably to race home if I throw to second. I check out the guy on first. He's big and looks slow. Maybe I can nail him.

I point down to Isaac, who taps his chest to indicate he's covering the base. I hold my glove a little higher. I'm going to have to move quickly.

Diego winds up and delivers a fastball. I leap out of my crouch as I catch it and throw as hard as I can to second. It's going to be close. Isaac grabs the throw and pulls his glove down for the tag.

"Out," the umpire hollers.

"Great throw, Jackson." Isaac pumps his fist.

"Good tag." I flip off my mask. "Let's get some runs."

As we crowd into the dugout, I spot someone running down the hill and see a flash of pink. Sydney. It's about time. Where in the world has she been?

CHAPTER 22

"I'm sorry, Coach Wilkins, my mom ran into another car and broke the taillight." Sydney's talking fast. "The other woman wasn't hurt or anything and neither was my mom—or me—but it took forever to get all the insurance information and then the police came and my mom couldn't leave, and I told the officer I had a baseball game, and he said, 'Softball,' and I said, 'Not softball. I play baseball.'"

"Slow down." Coach holds up his hands. "The important thing is that everybody is okay and that you're here."

Gig puts on a helmet and presses it down. He doesn't look at Sydney, but I can tell he's listening. I'm sure he's glad they're okay. And after watching Trenton nearly blow the last inning, he might even be glad to have her back.

"Sydney, warm up on the side with Trenton. You'll go in at second. Trenton, you'll move to right."

I grab a batting helmet and pick out my red bat.

"Batter up," the umpire hollers, and Gig steps to the plate.

I move into the on-deck circle and study the pitcher's motion. He's a short guy with a big leg kick, and he puffs out his cheeks before he releases the ball.

"Get us going, Gig," Isaac shouts.

Gig surprises everyone with a bunt down the first-base line and easily beats it out for a hit.

"Smart play," Coach shouts.

The first pitch is way inside and I jump back to avoid it. This guy is wild.

"Let's go, Jackson," G-Man calls.

The second ball is way high, and the third is outside.

"Make him pitch to you," Gig hollers from first.

I check with Coach in the third-base box and he rubs his eyebrow for the hit-away sign. If I like the pitch, I'm swinging.

"Way to work the count, Jackson," Isaac shouts.

The pitch is straight down the middle and I swing hard and smash a long fly to center. It's going to be out of here. My first home run. I watch the ball as I jog to first. The center fielder hurries back, and the ball smacks against the top of the fence and lands on the warning track. So close.

I put my head down and run hard. The center fielder fires the ball to second, and I slide in, barely avoiding the tag.

"Safe," the umpire hollers.

I bend down and pull up my leggings. That was close.

"Good hit," Diego hollers.

In the third-base box, Coach taps his head. "Jackson, remember to run everything out."

He's right. I should have been running hard, not watching the ball. Still, I brought Gig in. "Keep it going."

Isaac steps in and takes a couple of close pitches that the umpire calls for strikes.

"Protect the plate," Coach calls.

Isaac digs in. It must be strange to have your dad coach. Sometimes he's your dad, sometimes he's your coach. I'm sure Isaac didn't ask him to move to short. But he didn't say no or ask me what I wanted to do, either.

Isaac strikes out swinging on a pitch that's high.

"One out." Coach signals to me. "Go hard on a base hit."

Diego stands quietly in the batter's box. He looks so relaxed at the plate. No extra movements. Just his smooth, strong swing.

He takes a ball low and inside.

"Bring him home," Gig hollers.

The pitcher fires and Diego cracks a liner to left. I take off running and Coach is waving his arm like a windmill, signaling me to go for home. I make a tight turn and race for the plate. It's going to be close. I slide headfirst and reach out my hand.

"Safe," the umpire shouts.

I brush off my pants as my teammates pound me on the back. In the bleachers, Mom, Quinn, Ted, and the girls are standing and cheering.

"Nice slide." G-Man's clapping behind third.

"Good rip." Sydney holds out her hand and I slap it.

"Thanks." I don't care if Gig sees it or not. She's a teammate.

As soon as we take the field, the Leopards focus on Sydney.

"Girl at second."

"Check out her Barbie glove."

"They ran out of boys and had to get a girl for their team."

Sydney picks up a fast practice grounder from Gig and throws it back to him. She stretches her arms and acts like she doesn't hear the taunts, but of course, she does.

Isaac walks over and says something to her and she nods.

Diego fires his fastball and my glove pops.

"One more," the umpire says.

"Second," I call out. I catch the ball and fire to the bag, where Sydney grabs it and makes an imaginary tag on a base runner.

"She even caught it," one of the Leopards says.

"Maybe she's on the team to catch a guy."

"Check her out. That's the only way she'd get a boyfriend."

Gig paces back and forth at first base. How does he feel about these guys getting on his sister? It's one thing for him to tease her. It's something else for these jerks to do it.

The first batter smashes a sizzler to Sydney. She picks it up and fires to Gig for the out.

"Good play, Syd." I point to her. She doesn't miss much with that pink glove. Maybe it *is* lucky.

The second batter hits a blooper to right that Trenton manages to stay in front of. He throws the ball to second to hold the batter to a single.

"One down." I raise up my index finger. "Double-play time." G-Man is right about catching. I am more involved in each pitch, and I pay more attention to what everybody else is doing.

The next batter is the pitcher. He lifts his hand for time

and digs in at the back of the box. On the first pitch, he bunts down the first-base line. I throw off my mask and rush out, but Gig's charged in and picked up the ball. He turns and throws to Sydney, who's covering first. The runner is out, but he steps to the inside and runs into her. Sydney sprawls backward on the ground, but hangs on to the ball.

"What are you doing?" I rush out.

"You're out of the baseline." Isaac points at the runner.

"Just good, hard baseball," he says.

"Dirty baseball," I snap. "Play the game the right way."

Isaac and I offer a hand to pull Sydney up. "You okay?" he asks.

"Yeah." She picks up her hat.

She's tough. Even Gig, who's standing and watching, has to appreciate that.

It looks grim. We're behind by three and down to our last out. Even grimmer: Sydney's the batter. The Leopards' pitcher grins and rubs the ball in his hands. He's still firing bullets. I sit on the bench and wipe my forehead. I'm not going to get a chance to bat again.

On the first pitch, Sydney ducks to avoid another ball thrown at her head.

"C'mon, Syd," I holler. "Just get on."

The pitcher rears back and fires a fastball inside. Sydney doesn't even move this time, and the ball thwacks her on the thigh.

"Take your base," the umpire says, and Sydney jogs down with a smile.

"Way to take one for the team," I cheer. That's a tough way to get on base, but it keeps our chances alive.

Gig strides to the plate and glares at the pitcher. Is he mad because we're down by three or because the pitcher just hit his sister?

He swings at the first pitch and laces a single to center. Sydney races down to second and holds there.

"Batter up."

I'm up. I race to grab my bat and a helmet and hurry to the plate. Two on, two out. I need to keep the rally going.

The pitcher tries to tempt me with two fastballs outside, but I lay off both of them. The next ball is high. Three balls and no strikes. I turn to Coach, who gives me the take sign. I want to smack it, but he's right. Down by three. What's most important is another base runner.

I take a fastball down the middle.

Three and one. I've got to swing now, but Coach touches

his hat and brushes his chest, which means I have to take the pitch again. It's right down the middle and I lay off it. I can't stand it.

"Be aggressive," G-Man hollers. He must know I was given the take sign or I would have swung at that last pitch.

I step out of the box and look to Coach. He gives me the green light to swing away. Yeah, now that I've got two strikes on me. I take a practice swing and notice Mom talking with Ted and the girls. I dig in at the batter's box. I can't pay attention to them now. If I miss this pitch, the game is over.

The pitcher winds up and blazes a fastball outside. It's too close to take. I reach for it and hit a bouncer foul. I'm still alive.

"You can do it, Jackson." Mom claps.

The pitcher steps off the mound and wipes his hand on his pants leg. Finishing this game is tougher than he expected. He's probably regretting hitting Sydney right now.

I dig my back foot in and get ready. The next pitch comes in low. I start my two-strike swing but at the last moment pull my bat back.

"Ball four," the umpire calls. "Take your base."

"Way to go, Jackson," Gig hollers from second.

"Good eye," Sydney shouts from third.

Bases loaded for Isaac and we're still hanging on.

He takes a ball outside on the first pitch.

"Make him come to you," I shout.

On the next pitch, Isaac lines a shot down the right field line. I take off running. I might have a chance to tie it, but Coach holds up his hands to stop me at third. Two runs in. Guys mob Gig and Sydney, as Diego comes to the plate.

"Bring me home." I clap.

Behind by one and down to our last out. There's nobody I'd rather have batting.

The pitcher throws the first pitch high and Diego lays off. The second is outside for ball two. Diego takes his smooth practice swing.

"Let's go, Diego," Isaac calls from second.

The pitcher fires a fastball and Diego wallops it. I race for home with the tying run, but turn when I see their team cheering. The left fielder is standing at the fence holding up his glove with the ball in it. Third out, game over.

I plunge from excitement to disappointment in one second. I look over at my teammates, who are just as stunned.

"So close," Isaac says.

"I thought that was out of here."

"Not quite," he says.

Sydney kicks the fence and Gig throws his glove down. Tough loss, but something feels different. We played like a team.

Chapter 23

"*N*ow we *edit*." Hayes writes the word on the board. "After we have our story and after we do revision, now it's time to edit. Focus on punctuation, grammar, and spelling. Read your paper to yourself and circle any words you are unsure about."

I skim my paper. It's three typed pages. That's the longest paper I've written in a while.

"Check your spelling." Hayes walks among us. "You can't just rely on spell-check. Why not?"

"If it's another word, spell-check won't think it's wrong," Gig says.

Mrs. Spanier smiles.

"Exactly." Hayes puts his finger on my page. "You want the other kind of 'to,' don't you?"

"Yeah." I add another O.

"Mrs. Spanier and I will help out," Hayes says. "Raise your hand if you have a question."

I raise my hand to ask Hayes if I've done my quotation marks properly, but he's busy talking to Gig about commas. Instead I get Mrs. Spanier. "Are these quotation marks right?"

She bends down to examine my paper and I smell her lilac perfume. "This looks good, Jackson."

"Thanks."

"Some of these titles are lame." Hayes raises his hands in disbelief. "You've got these great stories about superheroes and the destruction of the world, but then you pick a boring title like 'My Adventure.'"

I look down at my title: "The Big Game."

"You've been in school so many years that you are used to these safe summing-up titles. It's not like you're writing a report on anteaters that you call 'Anteaters.'" He pulls his arms out wide. "You can stretch here. Put a number one next to your current title. Then read through your story and write down two other possible titles. The words for your title will often be found right there in your story."

I read through my pages looking for words that could work as a title. Nothing. Nothing. Then I find "Monster

Hit." That could be title two. "HOMERUNZILLA Carries His Tail" could also work.

"Once you have three titles, put a diamond next to the one you like best."

"Why a diamond?" Gig asks.

"I don't know." Hayes shrugs. "Because I like baseball?"

"If you like baseball, you should come to our next game," Gig says. "We play the Jaguars on Wednesday at Echo Park."

"I'll see," says Hayes. "Depends how my writing is going."

I say the three titles to myself and put a diamond next to number three.

"Anybody having trouble deciding which one is best?"

Gig raises his hand.

"Yes, Gig." Hayes walks over.

Mrs. Spanier looks up from helping Trenton with his spelling. "His given name is Spencer."

"I know," Hayes says. "I said I'd call students whatever they wanted to be called within reason. Gig's within reason."

Mrs. Spanier shakes her head and points to another word on Trenton's page.

Gig slides his paper to the side of the desk for Hayes to see.

"We need to play the Title Game," Hayes says. "Gig has

three titles for us and he'll read them out loud. After you've heard all three, vote for your favorite." He holds up his index finger. "Number one."

"'The Big Fight,'" Gig says.

"Number two."

"'After Dark.'"

"Number three."

"'I'm Going to Get You.'"

"As Gig reads them again, raise your hand for your favorite," Hayes says.

"The Big Fight" gets one vote.

"After Dark" gets three votes.

"I'm Going to Get You" wins by a landslide.

"See how we automatically know what makes a good title," Hayes says. "In these stories a little mystery in the title, a little uncertainty, is fine. We don't know who says, 'I'm going to get you,' but we want to read to find out."

After that, all kinds of kids raise their hands to play the Title Game. They read out their titles and we vote, and the one we choose is usually better than their first one.

"Anybody else?" Hayes asks.

I raise my hand and read out my three titles. "HOME-RUNZILLA Carries His Tail" wins by a mile.

"Yes," Hayes says. "We want to know why he carries his tail. A good title like that forces us to read the story. You all need to give yourselves room here. You need to give yourself permission to be creative."

"**F**ourteen days left." Gig dips his cheese bread in marinara sauce at lunch. "Then we're out of this prison."

I pick at my fruit cup. "And finished with these bad lunches."

"I like dunkers," Gig says. "Give me yours if you don't want it."

I hand him what's left of my dunker. He'll eat anything.

"Feel my finger." He holds it out. "I've got some kind of growth on it."

I reach out, and as soon as I grab it, he farts loudly.

I shake my head.

"What died?" Diego covers his nose.

"You're something." Isaac shakes his head at Gig, who just laughs.

Normally a guy farting at lunch would be kind of gross, but today it's good. The old Gig is back.

"I've got an announcement." Isaac holds up his hand.

We all stop eating and look at him.

"A change of plans. Next year for middle school, I'm not going to Eagle Bluff. I'm going to Longview!"

"Awesome." I reach out my fist for him to pound. "I thought your parents said you had to go to Chickadee Bluff because of the teachers."

"One of those teachers is transferring to Longview," Isaac says. "And I've been working on my folks. I persuaded them how important it is for me to stay with my friends."

"To Longview." Gig raises his chocolate milk.

"To Longview." I bump mine with his and Isaac's. "Diego, you're going to Longview, right?"

"Yeah."

"Then raise your milk for the toast," Gig says.

"Longview, Longview," we all chant together.

"We've got to stick together," I say. "It's even more important at middle school. Otherwise, those eighth graders will pick us off one by one."

I sit in front of the computer and read FutureMe messages. One guy tells his future self how important it is to stay connected with his old friends. A girl asks her future self if she is still going out with Anthony and reminds herself how bad he is for her. HE'S POISON. DUMP HIM IMMEDIATELY.

It's interesting what people want to tell themselves. One guy asks his future self to forgive him for all the dumb mistakes he made when he was young. Another says that the past selves don't disappear; they fade into ghosts who haunt your present decisions.

Some people write messages that are funny to themselves. Others are bossy. A few don't even expect to like their future selves and how they've turned out.

I click on Create New Entry and stare at the blank box. I think about what's happened with Gig, Isaac, Diego, and me. I think about Sydney, who I never thought I'd like, but who's turned out to be okay. I think about Mom and Dad and Quinn and G-Man. But most important, I want to warn my future self about a few things.

Warning to FutureMe,

Stay tight with Diego, Isaac, and Gig. Don't let anyone break up the group. Don't you do anything to break up the group. Do everything you can to keep things together.

Friends are even more important in middle school. Am I right?

Have you been beat up at Longview? Are the bullies as mean as you thought?

Is the homework bad? Are the teachers mean?

Have you gotten taller? Stronger?

You should go look at a picture of yourself from fifth grade to see how much you've changed.

Do you miss elementary school one tiny bit or are you glad to be gone?

Are the girls hot? Do you have a girlfriend yet? What's her name?

You rock,
Your fifth-grade self

P.S. Have you seen that ghost again?

I select a date that's six months away. It's too bad it's not possible to do it the other way around. Wouldn't it be great if my future self could send a message back to me about what I should do now?

CHAPTER 24

"**L**et's go, Panthers."

The bleachers are packed for our rematch with the Jaguars, who are tied for first place. I unwrap a piece of bubble gum and scan the spectators. Dad, Quinn, and G-Man are sitting across the way behind third base. Mom's sitting by herself behind home plate. No sign of Ted and the girls.

Quinn says something to Dad and Dad nods. Quinn runs over and sits next to Mom. Gig's folks hold hands and neither of them looks like they want to let go. Behind them, Isaac's mom knits the last sleeve of another sweater.

"Fire up." Gig claps. "Time for revenge."

I snap the straps of my catching gear. Everybody, other than Gig, seems unusually quiet as the Jaguars strut off the field after finishing their warm-ups. They act like they're the greatest team in the history of baseball.

"Look alive," Coach Wilkins says. "Hustle out to your positions."

I stand next to him behind the first-base line while he sprays grounders to the infielders. Sydney makes a nice stab of a bouncer and throws to Diego. He fires it to me and I flip to Coach.

"We're going to have to play our A-game to beat these guys," he says.

I look over at the Jaguars dugout. Guys point and laugh at Sydney. What's the big deal? They've already played us once. You'd think they'd be used to her being on our team by now.

"Batter up," the umpire hollers.

The first batter saunters to the plate and I squat down in my crouch. Gig focuses in and I give him a target outside. He throws and the batter hits a slow roller to second. Sydney charges in. She's going to have to hurry. She barehands the ball and bobbles it.

"Safe," the umpire shouts.

"She can't catch." The chatter starts from the dugout.

"Hit it to second."

"Hit it to the girl with the girly glove."

I glare at their dugout. Why doesn't their coach shut them

up? He's standing in the third-base coach's box with a grin on his face. Does he think it's funny?

I get back in my crouch and Gig delivers a ball inside.

"You can do it, Gig," Isaac calls.

On the next pitch, the runner smashes a ball up the middle. Sydney takes one step to her right, sticks out her glove, and grabs it. She flips to Isaac, who's crossing the bag, and he fires to Diego.

"Double play," I holler. "Good grab, Syd. Good throw, Isaac."

Gig slaps his glove. That's a huge play. Nobody on and two outs, rather than first and third and nobody out.

He throws two strikes and then gets the batter to chase a high one for strike three.

"Way to take him yourself, Gig," I holler. "Let's get some runs."

When Sydney comes to bat in the third inning, the game is still scoreless. Gig's pitching well, but their pitcher is throwing even harder.

"No batter." The third baseman smirks.

"Everybody move in," the shortstop calls.

The pitcher walks off the mound laughing as Sydney steps in.

"Start it off, Syd." I clap.

The pitcher takes a long stride and throws his first pitch underhand. His teammates burst out laughing.

"Ball one," the umpire calls.

What's going on? "Play the game right," I holler.

Coach Wilkins stares at their coach, who shrugs his shoulders like he can't do anything about it.

The pitcher throws another underhand pitch in his exaggerated motion.

"Ball two," the ump says.

"He's just trying to help you, batter," the first baseman says. "You should be playing softball."

Sydney digs in with hard kicks and I can tell she's mad.

"Let's go, Syd." Isaac claps. "You can do it."

"Take it to them," I shout.

"Slam it down their throats," Gig joins in.

"Maybe he's afraid to pitch to her." I hear a familiar voice in the stands.

Gig, Diego, Isaac, and I all turn to look. It's Hayes. I can't believe he's here at our game.

He points to us. "This is your inning."

The pitcher winds up the regular way and throws hard. Sydney swings and hits a ball down the first-base line. The first baseman, who's been mouthing off, isn't ready and the ball gets past him. Sydney races to first and our team explodes with cheers. Even Gig's clapping.

"Good hit," Diego shouts.

"Keep it going." I move to the on-deck circle and tighten the Velcro on my batting glove.

At first base, Sydney stands tall on the bag and rubs her hands together. "C'mon, Gig."

The pitcher throws a strike and Gig smacks it to right field for a hit. Sydney charges around second and steams to third when the right fielder bobbles the ball.

Runners at first and third with nobody out as I step in. I survey the field. The third baseman is playing deep and I have an idea.

The first pitch is low for ball one. The next pitch is inside and I stick my bat out and bunt it toward third. The ball rolls up the line as I race to first. The third baseman is slow to react and I beat it out by a mile as Sydney crosses home plate with our first run. The guys mob her and our fans go crazy. Her dad gives her mom a big hug and they're both beaming.

"Way to go, Jackson," Hayes shouts.

"Great bunt." Gig points at me.

"Smart play," G-Man calls from the stands.

I stand at first and soak up the cheers. The Jaguars are quiet. Scoring some runs is the best way to shut them up. "Keep it going, Isaac." I clap.

He digs in and whacks the first pitch for a single to left. Gig races around to score and I hold at second. Two to zero. The loudmouths look like they don't know what hit them.

"Your turn, Diego." I stand on the base. "Ducks on the pond."

"Meat on the table," Isaac shouts.

I look over at Coach to see if he's giving any signs. Behind him, G-Man is standing along the fence talking with a short man wearing a baseball hat pulled down low.

Diego takes three balls and Coach gives him the hit-away sign. The next pitch is down the middle and Diego's bat whips around. As soon as I hear the ping of the bat, I know it's gone.

I dance off of second and watch the ball soar over the right-field fence. I pump my arms as I jog home. "Five to nothing." I bump fists with Isaac as he comes to the plate, and everybody streams out of the dugout to congratulate Diego.

"You crushed it." I slap his back.

Diego breaks into the widest smile I've seen from him. He taps his chest and points to the man talking to G-Man.

"Who's that?" I ask.

"My dad. This is the first game of mine he's come to here. He used to play baseball in Mexico." Diego's face shines with joy.

So does Isaac's and Gig's and Sydney's. Mine, too.

This game is like that. When everything goes right, baseball feels better than anything.

CHAPTER 25

"**T**welve to five." I sit down at an outdoor table at A&W with Gig, Diego, and Isaac. "Sweet revenge. We won't have to listen to that Jaguar trash talk anymore."

"Those guys needed a good whipping." Isaac leans back in his chair.

"Stupid underhanded pitching." Gig shakes his head.

"That backfired on them." Diego stretches out his legs.

The waitress sets four mugs of root beer down on our table and I take a long drink. Root beer after a big win tastes so good.

"Thanks, Mr. Milroy," Isaac says to Gig's dad, who's treating.

"Yeah, thanks." I rub my sweaty forehead. I like how I feel after I've caught a game, like I've had a hard workout. Catching isn't better than shortstop, but it's close.

"My pleasure." Mr. Milroy waves. He sits with Sydney, Trenton, and Hauser, who lifts up his cast for Mr. Milroy to sign. Gig hasn't said anything more about his dad going away. It's got to be getting closer.

Between worrying about keeping the team together and thinking about Gig, my mind has been jumping all over. Right now it's nice to be here. Not the past me or the future me, just the present me, drinking root beer with the light breeze drying my sweat.

"You first four had nine hits, five walks, and seven runs batted in." Coach Wilkins studies the scorecard. "No errors, either. Terrific work."

"To the top of the order," Isaac says, and we all clunk our mugs together.

"All for one and one for all." Gig raises his other arm like he's carrying a sword.

"What?" Diego looks at him.

"We've got to stay together," Gig says.

"He's right." I tap the table. "Going to Longview, we need to stick together."

"For protection," Gig adds. "We've got to have one another's backs."

"And we should pledge right now to play on all the same teams," I say.

"Basketball." Isaac pretends to shoot a jump shot.

"Baseball." I raise my glove.

"Football." Gig smacks his fist.

Diego shakes his head. "I've never played football."

"Don't worry." Gig hits him on the shoulder. "You're big and we need you. You have to go out with us."

"Okay, but if I go out for football, you all have to do one thing for me this summer."

"Sure," I say. "What?"

"Soccer camp. I'm going in August with my cousin for a week, and I want all of you to come."

"No way." Gig holds up his hands like a criminal. "I don't play soccer."

"I don't play football," Diego says.

I shrug my shoulders. "He's got a point, Gig."

"But I hate soccer." Gig scowls.

"I'm not any good, either," I say. "But it's only a week. And it means we get Diego for baseball, football, and basketball. We need him. You said so yourself."

"Besides, if we're all going to stick together, we have to

stick together." Isaac spits into his hand and holds it out. "Four for four."

"Four for four." We each spit into our hand and slap with one another.

"We're tight like this." Gig jams the four fingers of his hands together.

"Yeah." I sit tall and stretch my hands out to Gig on one side and Diego on the other. They clasp hands with me and reach for Isaac. The fingers of our hands are linked together in a strong circle. Gig, Isaac, Diego, and me—the top of the order.

Acknowledgments

*T*hank you to my mother, Luanne Coy, who opened the world of books and all its possibility to me.

Thank you to the writers of KTM for their eagle eyes and ongoing encouragement.

Thank you to Liz Szabla and the team at Feiwel and Friends for their enthusiasm and support, and to my all-star agent, Andrea Cascardi.

Thank you to Jay Patrikios and Matt Sly for their great Web site: www.futureme.org. Check it out.

Thank you to everyone at Echo Park Elementary School. Particular thanks to Sally Soliday, Paula Kranz, Judy Zarn, the PTO, and to Dan Dudley and Kim Coleman and their fifth-grade students for their insights and suggestions.

And special thanks to my own fifth-grade teacher, Mrs. Garrison, of Manz Elementary School, who provided the initial connection to Echo Park. The circle comes round.

Thank you for reading
this **FEIWEL AND FRIENDS** book.

The Friends who made

TOP OF THE ORDER

possible are:

Jean Feiwel, publisher

Liz Szabla, editor-in-chief

Rich Deas, creative director

Elizabeth Fithian, marketing director

Barbara Grzeslo, associate art director

Holly West, assistant to the publisher

Dave Barrett, managing editor

Nicole Liebowitz Moulaison, production manager

Jessica Tedder, associate editor

Caroline Sun, publicist

Allison Remcheck, editorial assistant

Ksenia Winnicki, marketing assistant

· ·

Find out more about our authors and artists and
our future publishing at
www.feiwelandfriends.com.

OUR BOOKS ARE FRIENDS FOR LIFE